"So, you're from Gold Hill? Is that where your parents are from?"

"No," Madalyn said, feeling her forehead wrinkling. Even though her mouth almost opened to supply the answers of exactly where they were from, Madalyn stopped herself. That wasn't anyone's business. She added, uncertainly, "Um . . . why?"

Carlin gave Madalyn a long look, studying her face again. "Well, it's obvious you're not from around here," she said, and shrugged.

Tanita S. Davis

Partly Cloudy

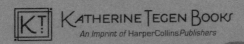
KATHERINE TEGEN BOOKS
An Imprint of HarperCollins Publishers

Katherine Tegen Books is an imprint of HarperCollins Publishers.

Partly Cloudy
Copyright © 2021 by Tanita S. Davis
Interior art © 2021 by Geneva Bowers

Library of Congress Control Number: 2021935516
ISBN 978-0-06-293701-8

Typography by Laura Mock
22 23 24 25 26   PC/CWR   10 9 8 7 6 5 4 3 2 1

First paperback edition, 2023

For everyone who already knows
there's never a bad time to be a good neighbor—
and to those just learning how—
you've got this.

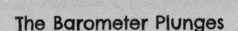

The Barometer Plunges

It should have been raining.

There should have been thick, slate-colored clouds piled up against a pewter-colored sky. There should have been sharp, cold winds whistling and silver-bright stabs of lightning.

Instead, it was a bright, sunny June-in-California morning, and Madalyn Thomas was cranky.

Normally on the first day of summer, Madalyn would have been pretty thrilled. Summer was for unlimited reading and eating all the strawberries she could fit into her mouth. Summer was for sleeping in and ice-cream trucks. But Madalyn wasn't prepared to be thrilled about summer just yet, because she was still thinking over the last school year.

Sixth grade had been *terrible*. Even before school began last August, things had started going wrong. First, Madalyn's dog, Lucy, had died. Then, her best friend, Avery, had moved far away to Winters. After that, Madalyn found out all the stomachaches she had were because she was lactose intolerant.

And then—on top of that? Madalyn's dad was laid off from the job he'd had for years and years. Madalyn and her parents had to move from their cozy-cute townhouse to an older house on the other side of town where the rent was less expensive. Madalyn had to change schools, too, and Robinson Howard Middle School wasn't even a little bit nice. It was big and gray, and the lights in the library had dead bugs in them. The cafeteria was huge, and without Avery, Madalyn never knew who to sit with. Her first day, there was a huge food fight—and she got spaghetti in her hair.

The day a kid named Mark brought a gun in his backpack to show around was the *worst*. People were screaming. Teachers were panicking. Madalyn forgot everything she had learned in shooter drills and ran out of the cafeteria into the bathroom and hid on a toilet seat, choking down sobs and hoping no one came in.

Madalyn survived the school year—and Lucy dying and Avery moving and never having dairy ice cream again without taking a pill. But she was determined never, ever, ever, *ever* to go back to Robinson Howard Middle School again.

Which her mom said was fine.

"What do you mean, it's fine?" Madalyn blurted, twisting around in her seat at the table.

"It's been a rough year for all of us, babe," Mom said, tilting the pan and swirling the eggs as they cooked. She looked up and flashed Madalyn a smile, her brown cheeks dimpling. "Skies are clearing, though. Your dad and I have a plan."

Great. Madalyn rolled her eyes. She knew all about Mom and her weather metaphors. "The winds of change are blowing" was what she'd said when she'd told Madalyn they were leaving Gold Hill. "Your dad and I have a plan" was Momspeak for "we're changing something else"—and change wasn't something Madalyn wanted to deal with at seven a.m. on a Sunday. She was only up at that hour because Daddy was catching a flight to Cambridge in Massachusetts for a Monday job interview, and Mom wanted the family to eat together before he left. As soon as he was on the way to the airport, Madalyn was going back to bed.

She yawned and gave in to her curiosity. "What plan, Mom? Robinson Howard is the only middle school around here." That was true, not counting the local girls' Catholic school, Sacred Heart. Madalyn loved their sharp blazers and tartan skirts but hadn't liked the idea of wearing white knee socks every single day, just like two hundred other seventh-grade girls. Now Madalyn kind of wished she were Catholic, just a little. Blazers, at least, weren't bullets.

"It's going to take strategy and a little more team-work," Mom said, putting the hot skillet on the metal trivet to protect the tabletop, "but there might be another option for next year."

Madalyn straightened. "What option? You're going to teach me at home?"

"Oh, no thanks," Mom said, laughing. "You're too smart for me already. Listen, babe—don't worry about it, all right? Something is going to work out, just wait and see."

Madalyn sighed. She hated waiting for anything. Fortunately, just then Madalyn's father rolled his luggage into the kitchen, and then there was sourdough toast, eggs, and sliced avocado to distract her.

Ten minutes after she'd hugged and kissed her father

and stood in the driveway to wave goodbye, Madalyn was back under her snuggly flannel comforter and cuddling down with a book when she heard the house phone ring. She almost didn't answer it. No one ever called the landline except robocallers and people asking questions about politics. Mom and Daddy didn't use it—they always had their cell phones. But Madalyn got nosy and got up after the phone rang three times.

"Thomas residence," she said, a little winded from her dash across the hall.

"Macie? Where's my worthless *neveu*? How come he don't call me on my birthday?" The voice was strident.

"This is Madalyn, not Macie," Madalyn corrected. "Mom's not here right now. Is this—?"

"Ooh, little Madalyn! You sound just like your *mamm*! How you doing? This your Papa Lobo, so where's that daddy of yours?"

"I thought it was you!" Madalyn grinned. Papa Lobo was Madalyn's great-uncle, the brother of her grandfather Collin—or Grandpa Collie, as the cousins had called him since they were small. Papa Lobo had followed his brother to California when they were young men, and though Grandpa Collie had gone home to

Louisiana when he retired, Papa Lobo was still a couple of hours away in Sheldon.

"How are you, Papa Lobo?"

"How you think I am? I'm seventy-three. I'm an old, old man, *ché*," he said, and Madalyn felt giggles rising at his tone.

"Happy birthday, old, *old* man," Madalyn teased. "I'm sorry, but Daddy's not here. He's on his way to the airport. He's got another interview."

"Oh, that's right, that's right. Well, I guess I'll have to wait on him to call me, then," the old man said. "You tell him to call me when he gets home, you hear?"

"You don't have to wait," Madalyn said quickly. "You have his cell number, right? Or you can send him an email. He'll get it on the plane."

"Don't matter," Papa Lobo said abruptly. "I got to go; I got my poker game. You be sweet, Madalyn, and tell that mama of yours I said hey."

The line disconnected, and Madalyn kept smiling as she hung up. She didn't know her great-uncle that well, but she liked Papa Lobo. He was a little . . . different than most people. Papa Lobo wrote letters on paper and didn't use a computer. He read a paper newspaper all the way through, and listened to talk shows on the radio, and he didn't text, ever. Instead of driving his truck all the time like most adults, he rode a wide-tired bicycle with a big basket around his town instead. Mom said it was because he was a small-town nonconformist and had done things his way forever. Madalyn thought Papa Lobo just liked to be contrary, as Grandpa Collie put it. Madalyn knew Papa Lobo wouldn't call Daddy back, that was for sure; Daddy would have to call him, or Papa Lobo would never let him hear the end of it.

Later that evening when Daddy called from his hotel in Cambridge, her mother put the call on speaker, and Madalyn passed her message along. "Daddy, you forgot Papa Lobo's birthday."

Madalyn heard her father's breath exhale in a hiss. "Ah, man! I remembered this morning, but I forgot already. Thanks." He paused. "So, you had a nice talk with him? What's going on with the old boy?"

"No. We didn't talk for very long," Madalyn said. "He said he had poker."

Daddy snorted. "Poker. He cheats, you know that? That's how he always wins. Him and those old dudes he plays with all cheat, the lot of them."

Madalyn giggled. Papa Lobo had inherited a couple of Grandpa Collie's old friends and turned them into a poker club. "He should move to Louisiana. Grandpa

Collie says he and his retired friends play all week."

"Nah, Uncle Lo won't go back. He says he can't see the sense of hurricanes every year. Guess he likes earthquakes just fine." Daddy laughed.

"We'll drop by and see him tomorrow night for dinner," Mom said, rejoining the conversation.

"Good idea," Daddy said. "Take Madalyn over, bring him a birthday cake, and make him eat a salad so he can complain about it. I'd better call him before I forget again," Daddy said.

Madalyn grinned. She didn't really mind salad, but hearing Papa Lobo complain about the way Mom was vegetarian and she "didn't eat enough to keep body and soul together" was pretty funny. As long as Madalyn knew there was cake, hanging out with Papa Lobo was just fine with her.

Mom turned the car around at the end of the street and parked in front of the slightly worn gray ranch house with the long porch and dusty laurel bushes clustered before the front windows. The old man threw open the front door the moment the car stopped at the curb. Papa Lobo was whip thin and gnarled like a piece of aged mahogany, and his dark brown face had smile lines and deep wrinkles around his eyes, the same as Daddy. As always, he wore a ball cap and was chewing gum. Like Grandpa Collie, he grew up in southern Louisiana, which gave him a soft drawl and lots of funny sayings.

His arms were like steel wires, and his hug nearly dented Madalyn's ribs. "C'mon in, c'mon in out the heat," Papa Lobo boomed, exclaiming at Madalyn's height, her round face—"*Mamzèl,* look just like her old daddy"—and her mass of crinkled dark hair, which was pulled into a ponytail. After hugs and whiskery, coffee-scented kisses, the old man took the big chocolate cake Mom had brought and led them into the front hall with satiny striped wallpaper, a skinny-legged table holding a pendulum clock, and pale wood floors. He opened a pair of glass-paneled accordion doors to a cool, dim room and waved them inside. "Come sit down in the front room! I'll just put this cake in the icebox."

As Papa Lobo disappeared toward the kitchen, Mom smiled and made a game show gesture toward the open doors. "Ooh, we're special today! The company room!"

"I know, right?"

Madalyn had been to Papa Lobo's several times since he'd moved to Sheldon, but she'd never gotten to sit in the front room. The glass-paneled accordion doors to that space were always closed, and the curtains were pulled tight over the big picture window. An empty room had never seemed particularly interesting to Madalyn—they mostly visited Papa Lobo when Grandpa Collie was in town, and then the noise and fun was centered in the kitchen, where the food was. Now Madalyn stepped into the dim space behind her mother, silent and curious.

She took a breath of the cool, slightly flowery-scented air and plopped down beside her mother, only to leap up again as the couch beneath her crinkled unpleasantly.

"Eeeew! Mom, we're sitting on plastic." Madalyn's legs, bare in her shorts, separated from the couch's clinging surface with a sucking sound.

"I know," Mom said, sounding amused. "Just pull the legs of your shorts down a little, and you won't stick so much."

Madalyn frowned, sitting carefully. "What's with the plastic-wrapped everything?"

"People do that to keep things nice in humidity," Mom said.

"Wouldn't plastic make it worse?" Madalyn wondered aloud.

As funny and special as Papa Lobo was, his front room wasn't very special at all. It was . . . *ugly*. When it was new, it had probably been a very fancy room. The floors were dark wood, with a thick, tasseled carpet on the floor between the long couches. There was a pretty chandelier in the middle of the ceiling, with prisms dangling down that would catch the light when it was on. The back wall had wallpaper that showed hundreds of trees in a dense tangle of trunks and golden leaves. It looked like a gigantic postcard. The other three walls had wood panels on them, which made the room look like a dark, foresty cave. And on every end table, on shelves, and clustered along a marble-topped table were hundreds of . . . roosters.

It was ridiculous. Some roosters were small and smooth, carved of wood, while others were brightly colored ceramic. Still others were made out of shellacked seashells, plaster, and blown glass. A calcified rock of hard candy sat in a covered rooster dish on the end table. Madalyn wondered if her great-uncle was like a person with too many cats, only he had too many roosters.

At least they weren't alive.

When she noticed the rooster embroidery on the couch pillows beneath the plastic, Madalyn jerked her eyes away. The sheer white curtains, plastic-covered floral couches, and all ten thousand roosters were covered with a thin layer of dust. And what was that flowery smell? Potpourri?

"Mom? Can we open a window?" Madalyn whispered. "I think something's giving me allergies."

Mom peeled herself carefully from the couch and tugged back the curtains. Madalyn sneezed as the blinds snapped up, teary-eyed and light-blind from the cool green light of the afternoon sun through the heavily overgrown trees.

"Not sure that's an improvement," said a voice behind her.

Madalyn jumped up. All she could see, with the afterimages of the light in her eyes, was a silhouette, but it was probably tall enough to block out the sky. She blinked and sneezed into the crook of her arm. "Excuse me. Who—?"

"Move, babe." Mom tugged on her arm, and Madalyn stumbled back a few steps, realizing the person was a skinny Black boy with short, prickly hair holding a tray with a pitcher while she squinted at him.

"Let me just set down *Paren*'s sweet tea," the boy said, then wiped his hands on his shorts. "I'm Jean

Duval. I live up the road. *Paren* might have mentioned me?"

Madalyn shook her head, staring. Jean—he said his name a little like "Jon"—looked about Madalyn's age, but his voice was so deep, so he was probably older, maybe in high school. Jean wore a faded brown T-shirt and baggy denim shorts, and Madalyn stared at his shoes—which were huge. He was tall—taller than Mom, too, which Madalyn found a little annoying since he wasn't even an adult. She wondered why Jean thought Papa Lobo would have mentioned him.

Madalyn's mother reached past Madalyn to shake the boy's hand. "It's so nice to meet you, Jean," she said, giving Madalyn a look with raised eyebrows.

Oh. "Um, nice to meet you," Madalyn mumbled hurriedly, relieved when Papa Lobo bustled in with a plate of peanut butter cookies. The man stopped short and frowned around the room.

"Always forget about them cockerels," he muttered, and shook his head. "You all met *mon fiyo*, then. Boy, this is Macie Thomas, my nephew's wife, and his girl, Madalyn. Ladies, this is Jean Baptiste Duval; met his daddy when he was a young man in the service, that's one of the reasons I moved all the way out here. The boy's family."

Papa Lobo smiled and set about pouring the tea while Madalyn carefully settled next to her mother on the couch and translated Papa Lobo's drawling Louisiana Creole words. *Fiyo?* Must be "godson," since he'd called Papa Lobo his *paren*, a word Madalyn knew meant "godfather."

"It's nice to have some young people around, I'm sure," Mom said, smiling with a wrinkle of concern on her forehead. "But what did you mean you'd forgotten about the roosters, Uncle Lorenzo? How is your memory?"

Startled, Madalyn glanced at her mother. Mom's job was working with older people in retirement homes who needed someone to help get what they needed— did Papa Lobo need help, too?

But Papa Lobo gave a shout of laughter, his dark eyes wreathing with happy wrinkles. "Now, don't you worry none about this old man."

As Mom and Papa Lobo continued chatting, Madalyn took a sip of tea, which was icy cold and so very sweet it made her teeth hurt. Papa Lobo still made Louisiana sweet tea, like the kind she had at Grandpa Collie and Miss Peach's house. Papa Lobo explained how the roosters had come with the house while Madalyn sucked her aching teeth and studied Jean Duval in sneaky glances. Jean had already eaten three cookies but had left his tea alone. That was probably smart.

It really was unfair that Jean was so tall, with long arms and legs, and so skinny that his boots looked big. Madalyn wondered if he'd stopped growing already or if he was still growing. Boys grew fast, she knew. She wondered if she would ever be tall like—

"Ought to take a picture, *ché*, it'd last longer," Papa Lobo suggested, and Madalyn jerked.

"What?"

"Oh, I see you eyeing that dish. You go on ahead and have some candy."

What?! "Oh, um—" Madalyn shot her mother a frantic look, desperate not to have to chip away an ancient clump of rock-hard sugar. Lifting the iridescent glass rooster head, she peered in at the candy and poked it experimentally. "I, uh . . ." There was no polite way out.

Abruptly, Papa Lobo cackled, slapping his bony knee. "Shoulda seen your face, *ché*! Don't nobody in their right mind want to eat hundred-year-old candy.

I'm just teasing you. You have yourself a cookie and tell me why you want to move in with an old man like me."

Madalyn almost dropped the rooster head. Eyes wide, she twisted to stare at her mother, who looked, just then, a little like she'd had some of that old candy—and broken her tooth.

"Mom?" Madalyn said.

Someone needed to explain this to Madalyn—quick.

Gray Cloud Number Four

"We wanted to talk it over with Papa Lobo first," Mom said as she brought the car to a stop at the bottom of Papa Lobo's street.

"Huh." Madalyn stared down at her fingers tapping a fast rhythm against the seat belt buckle. *Tap-a-tap-tap-tap. Tap-a-tap-tap-tap.* That was the rhythm of her heart, maybe, or the swish-swirl of the spin cycle going on in her stomach. She still couldn't work out how she was feeling.

"This wasn't our first choice. We tried applying for an inter-district transfer, so we could look at another school closer to where I work, but the district approves the requests only when there are spaces available—and there isn't space right now, plus there's a waiting list a mile long. We looked at Sacred Heart, but the tuition is more than we're comfortable with."

Her mother paused, but Madalyn didn't know what to say. She jerked a shoulder in a shrug.

"The Highland County School District has open enrollment, but a residency requirement—you would need to reside in Sheldon at least four days a week. You would come home on the weekends, of course," her mother went on. "Your father and I would come and pick you up as soon as the traffic died down. Or maybe you could take a bus after school."

"Uh-huh." Madalyn's tapping sped up.

"Nothing has been decided yet," Mom added, pulling into the quiet intersection and heading down a tree-lined road. "And it won't be, not until we see if your daddy gets this job in Massachusetts, but let's just take a look, Madalyn, all right?"

"Uh-huh," Madalyn said, but she didn't stop looking at her hands. *Tap-tap-tap. Tap-a—*

Mom exhaled a long sigh. "I know it's not an ideal situation," she admitted. "Uncle Lo doesn't have Wi-Fi yet, and he plays poker every week. I don't know about you hanging around old men with all that cigar smoking and swearing. But I also don't think either one of us can take another two years of Robinson Howard, can we? And, you know, Mads, this might be good for your great-uncle. He's getting up there a bit—you could help him out around the place a little. God knows something needs to be done about that front room."

"Huh," was all Madalyn could think to add. She nibbled her thumbnail. Living with Papa Lobo . . . well. Madalyn wasn't sure if the swirling she felt inside meant she was excited or sick. Her whole brain felt frozen.

A moment passed, and then Mom said, "Well, they have a cute little library, anyway."

Madalyn forced herself to look away from her fingers and saw a friendly-looking U-shaped brick building with an ornamental fountain out front, surrounded by gingko trees with yellow-green fan-shaped leaves. Madalyn looked more closely, noticing a senior center shared the parking lot. "Where's the middle school?" she managed.

"They don't have one." Mom glanced over at Mada- lyn, then braked at another stop sign. "It's a junior high—seventh to ninth grades. See?" As they crossed the intersection, her mother slowed the car and pointed. On one side of the road were tennis courts behind high fences, long, low buildings, and a parking lot with a tall digital sign announcing in bright blue letters that it was Sheldon High School, Home of the Vikings—and that it was 86 degrees Fahrenheit. Across the road on the other side was a neat line of bushes in front of a two-story brick building bearing its own sign. "Kingsbridge Junior High," Madalyn read, twisting to look at the flags fluttering lazily.

As her mother turned in to the parking lot, Madalyn practically pressed her face against the glass. Something slowed the spinning in her stomach and shifted the squish and swish farther up, into her chest. Her heart squeezed—with envy. Kingsbridge had a green lawn—Watered with Recycled Water, the sign said—painted brick planters, and flowers. Robinson Howard had been all gray brick boxes and not much green, except for the turf on the football field. Certainly nothing like flowers grew there. Judging by the number of crosswalks they had passed, kids who went to Kingsbridge could walk to school. Kids who walked to Kingsbridge could walk to school and right past the library every day. Madalyn could almost imagine attending a school like that—it probably had its very own school library, lots of clubs, electives, and maybe honors classes. Except for the wide accessibility ramps that curved like parentheses around the sides of the central stairway, the school looked like it could have been in use hundreds of years ago.

"It's all pretty," Madalyn said finally as her mother made a U-turn and headed back the way they'd come. "Do you think it's a good place?" Robinson Howard hadn't looked like it was a bad school from the outside. Madalyn didn't trust what she couldn't see anymore.

"I think so," Mom said. "I've already talked to the front office staff, and they definitely have room for new students. There are less than nine hundred kids in the whole school, and each classroom has about thirty kids. I think it might have potential, don't you?"

Madalyn hedged. "I don't know . . . did Papa Lobo sound like he wanted me to move in with him?"

Madalyn couldn't tell. Papa Lobo had clearly been amused that Madalyn hadn't known what he was talking about, and that he'd gotten to spill the beans. He'd teased her about catching flies with her mouth open and Jean Duval had laughed—until Madalyn had snapped her mouth closed and glared at him.

"Yes, I do," Mom said slowly, sounding like she was thinking it over. "He *said* he'd be tickled to have you, at least. He's all by himself in that big old house, and I think it might be nice for the two of you to spend some time together—he must be a little lonely. But he's never had a daughter." Mom gave Madalyn a quick smile. "It would be an adjustment for both of you."

"Hmm." Madalyn frowned, her thoughts circling around and around. Papa Lobo hadn't ever had children—he hadn't gotten married, either, as far as Madalyn knew. Was that because he was secretly an awful person and nobody wanted to marry him? But Jean Duval's father liked him well enough to let Jean go over to visit with him—but that didn't mean anything. Maybe Jean was awful, too.

As if she'd read Madalyn's mind, her mother added, "And it'll be nice to have Jean around, too. He's probably a little older, but he'll know some people and can help you get acquainted. And he can help Papa Lobo get up to speed with stuff like Wi-Fi and computers and that kind of thing."

Madalyn wrinkled her nose. "*If* I move in with Papa Lobo."

"Yes," Mom agreed firmly. "All of this is still a big *if*. There's definitely still a lot of discussion that needs to happen between if and when."

Madalyn's next words were going to be "uh-huh" again, but her phone let out the fairy-dust chime reserved for text messages from Avery. Madalyn dug out her phone and whooped.

"Mom! Avery's going to family camp at Bishop Ranch for two weeks! Mrs. Fargas is going to call and ask if I can go! Can I? There's going to be fireworks on the Fourth! Say yes! Please!"

Mom grinned. "You're abandoning me already?" she teased.

Madalyn hugged her phone to her chest. "Avery says the water is high enough for canoeing." She sighed. "It's going to be *amazing*."

An excited Madalyn returned home to dig out her camping gear and line up her favorite books to swap with Avery during the first two weeks of July. Bishop Ranch was way up in Northern California, in the middle of rolling hills near Winters where a branch of Dry Creek met Lytton Lake. It was in a woodsy area, so Madalyn was looking forward to doing fun, woodsy things like playing in the water, digging to find geodes, and singing by the campfire. The Fargas family had been going to Bishop Ranch for years, and Madalyn was excited to still be invited. She'd hoped she would still be welcome, even though Avery had made new friends.

* * *

Madalyn hugged her mother tightly the Sunday morning she left for Avery's house. She promised herself that after kicking off her summer with Bishop Ranch, everything about her experiences at Robinson Howard would be a faint, bad memory—and then space in her brain would be cleared to sit down with Mom and Daddy and talk about what to do next school year.

But the talking and thinking didn't really happen—instead, *summer* did.

Daddy got a six-month job at a biopharmaceutical company in Cambridge, and the weekend before Madalyn got back from camping, Mom flew to Cambridge to help Daddy move. After that, Madalyn got her first real summer job, two long weeks of being a nanny for five hours a day. She came home every afternoon from that job exhausted—with no desire to do any thinking about anything.

And then it was the end of July, and Madalyn spent the weekends Daddy was home going out to the farmers' market, making trips to the library, and staying in and binge-watching all the shows and movies she'd wanted to see during the school year. The days fluttered by like dry seed pods, and Madalyn mostly forgot to worry about school . . .

Until she woke up one Friday and it was the first week of August.

"Your dad's coming home tonight," her mother announced that morning, tilting up the blinds in Madalyn's tiny bedroom before she carefully sat down on the edge of the bed in her nice linen work pants. "I need you to make sure to run the dishwasher after you eat and keep the house tidy today, please. Uncle Lo's coming for dinner to discuss how we're going to manage next year."

"W-What?" Madalyn sputtered, suddenly far more awake.

Her mother gave her a sympathetic look. "Yeah, summer just blew by, didn't it?" She looked more closely at her daughter. "I think you need a trim this weekend; your hair was looking a little wild yesterday. And it's probably time for new shoes. Again." She sighed, a big gusty breath, and moved to stand.

"Mom, wait! I don't know about this," Madalyn blurted, gripping her mother's arm. "We were going to talk about it, and . . . and . . ." She sucked in a panicked breath. "Are you sure we can't do homeschool? I swear, I'll get all the work done."

"Babe, when would I be home to work with you?"

Her mother sat back on the bed and looked pointedly at the watch on the arm Madalyn was holding. "I have six facilities to visit today. It's seven forty-five, and I have to be on the road in fifteen minutes. If you did homeschool through the district, you'd be by yourself all day from now until five fifteen, staring at a screen. Especially with Avery gone, you wouldn't have anyone to talk to. I don't think that's best for you, Madalyn, I really don't. You need people and friends, and to get out of your room sometimes."

People? Friends? Madalyn had no idea where she'd find those, spending all day with strangers at a new school in a new town, and all evening in a house full of roosters and a nice old man who didn't really know who she was, or what she liked to eat, or how late she liked to sleep, or what books she liked to read. . . . It was going to be weird—they were going to think *she* was weird. Who else lived with their great-uncle? Everyone else had parents, or at least grandparents, or something close. Papa Lobo was old, and he was a *great*-uncle, not even a normal one. She couldn't do this.

Madalyn swallowed tears. "I know, Mom, I just . . ."

"Hey. Hey, now." Her mother's expression softened. "What's the worst thing that could happen?"

Madalyn squirmed. Madalyn hated her mother's Worst Thing questions—they were even worse than the weather metaphors. She could think of far too many awful things, and unlike her mother's orderly imagination, which shooed unlikely events out of the way in a businesslike fashion, Madalyn's brain held on to all her worst things and made them bigger and gave them fangs, which did nothing to ease Madalyn's mind in the least. "I don't know," she mumbled finally, stalling.

"Think about that today," her mother said, bending to press a quick kiss to the crown of her head as she stood. "Think about the thing that you fear the most, and then we'll talk about how you can weather it when I get home. And don't forget what I said about the kitchen. If you're feeling extra ambitious, you can unload the dishwasher and set the table for me."

"'Kay," grunted Madalyn, pulling the covers up to her chin. Ambitious was the last thing she was feeling right now, but she knew Mom would ask her to do chores that evening if she didn't do them during the day.

A few minutes later, Madalyn heard the jingle of keys. "Bye! Don't stay in bed all day!" her mother called.

Madalyn made a face. "Bye, Mom," she called back, promising nothing.

"Get some exercise, babe. Step into the sunshine! It's a nice, bright, sunshiny day!"

"Okay, Mom, *goodbye*," Madalyn said, louder this time. She knew things were about to get bad if Mom started on song lyrics. "Jeez."

When the door finally closed, Madalyn flung herself back onto the bed and pulled the covers up over her face. "Aaaargh," she groaned. She wasn't ready for *any* of this.

Low Clouds and Fog

Her day had begun so perfectly—with scrambled eggs and a lopsided, heart-shaped pancake breakfast in bed in her big new bedroom at Papa Lobo's.

It was the *best* room. Papa Lobo's house was old, but old houses sometimes had neat surprises like built-in bookshelves and big closets. Madalyn's room had high ceilings, a big window that looked out over the backyard, and yellowy-pale pine floors. When Mom had come in with her breakfast, she hadn't even had to bring Madalyn a TV table—she'd just set the tray down next to Madalyn on the bed. Her new bed was *way* bigger than her old one at home.

"No way!" Madalyn had cheered, groping for her

phone. Mom hardly ever made pancakes, and never on a weekday. She snapped a quick picture and shared it with Avery.

Chuckling, Mom had brought in her tea and sat on the end of the bed, squeezing Madalyn's foot. "Don't take too long admiring your food, Mads," she said. "You still have to get ready, and you'll want to tidy up in here before you go."

"I will," Madalyn had promised, digging into her eggs. "It'll just take a minute."

Of course, even with showering the night before, it hadn't exactly been a *minute*. Tension had wound tighter and tighter as first one thing, then another, went wrong. Madalyn's hair looked stupid the way she'd first fixed it, which meant she'd taken another ten precious minutes to comb it out and braid it up into a princess braid. Then she'd put on her capris, but she changed shirts four times—from pale pink to floral to white to black with flowers—and that had taken more time. Then in all the half-unpacked clutter in her new room, she thought she'd lost her bike helmet—which had freaked her out entirely, because without her helmet, Mom wouldn't have let her ride her bike at *all*. Finally, she'd pulled herself together, dug out the helmet from the pile of stuff on the padded chair by the closet, shoved her snack into her backpack, and put on her helmet and shoes. Then Mom had gotten Daddy on speakerphone, and while he told her to have a good day, Mom had gotten all shiny-eyed. Mom was *not* the crying one in the family, so even with her eyes a little shiny she'd also almost made Madalyn cry—then Madalyn had maybe cried a little for real while she waved until her mother's car disappeared around the corner. Then Madalyn had had to splash water on her face and press a towel against her eyes until they looked better. Then she'd had to put on her sparkly lip gloss. Again.

Now Madalyn hesitantly dabbed the painful edges of her scrape and sighed. Papa Lobo had *said* she was going to be late. He'd *said* she should have gone earlier with Jean. Madalyn grimaced in pain and then scowled again, thinking about it. As if she were a baby who needed someone to help her cross the street!

Madalyn had leapt onto her bike in a rush. She could ride like the wind when she had to, and she did—up the block and around the corner to the stop sign, down the straightaway, avoiding the speed bumps, and then into the junior high parking lot, which was still edged by the pretty flowering shrubs Madalyn had seen when Mom had driven her past the school at the beginning of the summer. She hadn't been late—she'd arrived fifteen minutes before school started, and there were still people on the front lawns and in the parking lot . . .

Which is why there had been plenty of people around to see Madalyn hastily lock up her bike, grab her bag, and . . . trip over the curb and fall hard on her left knee.

Ouch.

Madalyn leaned against the wall of the bathroom stall and pressed her eyes. She couldn't sink down on the bathroom floor—*ick*—and cradle her poor battered leg, and she couldn't wear her sunnies in the classroom, so no matter how humiliated she felt, she absolutely could *not* cry. This was her brand-new start, and she wasn't going to begin the year sobbing in the bathroom. Throat tight, she pressed the wad of towels against her leg, hissing as the pain shivered up from where the skin had broken. She wondered if this was enough of an emergency to call her mother at work. Probably not—it was just a scrape, and plus, today was a minimum day, so she could go home an hour after lunch. She was fine.

It was just so *embarrassing*. As soon as she'd fallen, she'd heard calls of "Are you okay?" and had waved them away, limping into the nearest bathroom to repair the damage as fast as she could. Once she'd been hidden in the stall and her heart had stopped pounding so hard, she'd surveyed the road rash on her leg and winced. *Ugh*.

She was sweaty and shaky, and her leg was on fire, but she was fine. In just a minute, she would take a deep breath, snap a picture of her scraped-up leg, and shoot an ironic/funny text to Avery, reapply her lip gloss, and go to class.

In a minute.

An alarm on Madalyn's phone vibrated, sounding like a tiny, angry bee trapped in a minuscule glass jar. Madalyn winced. Ten minutes. She didn't want to be late. At Robinson Howard, being late was *horrible*. They'd had assigned seats, but people who were late had to sit in the corridor on a bench outside the door, and the teacher only let them in after she'd taken attendance. If the student coming into the room didn't have a pass, sometimes the teacher didn't let them in. Madalyn did *not* want to be late her first day at Kingsbridge Junior High.

Normally, Madalyn didn't care where she sat—especially now that Avery was at another school, it didn't matter. But right now, all she could think about was where she was going to sit and what everyone was going to see when she limped into the classroom while everyone looked. Late! On the very first day! She *hated* that Papa Lobo had been right after all. Madalyn wished she could text her mother right now—but Madalyn could count on one hand the number of times her mother had come and gotten her from school when she'd gotten hurt. And now she was too far away.

Madalyn dabbed her leg again, then set her jaw and pressed harder against the scrape. Pinkish water dribbled down her ankle, and Madalyn scowled. This was the *worst*.

The outer door of the bathroom swung open, and Madalyn heard heels click across the tiled floor. She jumped as a tap sounded against her stall door.

"Um, hello?" Madalyn stepped back and swallowed hard. Now what?

"How's your knee?" asked a brisk adult voice.

Hesitantly, Madalyn unlocked the stall and stepped out. A short woman with pale skin and a bubble of dark blond curls was holding a white first aid box next to the sink. She frowned down at Madalyn's leg. "Ouch. Do you want a bandage, or do you just want to spray it with antiseptic and go on to class?"

Madalyn didn't know what to say. "Um . . ."

The woman opened the first aid box and slipped a

pair of gloves out of a pocket of her polka-dotted tan dress. "Sorry. I'm Mrs. Dunston, school nurse here. Tug up that pant leg a little higher for me?"

"Okay. Um, I'm . . . I don't want to be late," Madalyn said, not really sure she wanted some stranger touching her. "It's fine."

"I'm sure you are," Mrs. Dunston agreed. She gestured Madalyn toward the sink. "Let me take a look at you anyway. Are you new this year?"

"Yes, ma'am," Madalyn said, wincing as Mrs. Dunston pulled out a plastic bottle from her metal box and held it up.

"This is just clean water," she said, and squirted it at Madalyn's knee, dabbing the extra away with a thick square of gauze.

Madalyn sucked in a pained breath as Mrs. Dunston squirted another stream of water over her scrape. "At least my capris didn't rip," she muttered.

"They're tougher than they look. Do you remember how to get to your class?" Mrs. Dunston pulled a green-and-white can from her kit and shook it.

"Yes," Madalyn said again, then sucked in another quick breath as Mrs. Dunston sprayed two short, freezing-cold blasts of antiseptic liquid against her skin.

"Well, then, you're good to go," Mrs. Dunston said, pulling off the gloves and stepping back. "If you hurry, you won't be late."

Madalyn gingerly tugged her pant leg down and grabbed her backpack. "Thanks. Did someone . . . send you to find me?"

Mrs. Dunston closed her first aid kit and shooed Madalyn toward the door. "Oh, no! There's a window in the front office—we all saw you fall. Off you go, now."

Wincing, Madalyn limped out into the breezeway. So much for blending in her first day.

People were still standing up and talking by the time Madalyn found the open door of Room 8 and slipped inside. Relieved, she tucked herself into an empty desk in the third row—the back row and the second-to-back row were filled—and looked around at the high-ceilinged room with the windows lining the wall and the cool tile underfoot. Madalyn could feel the buzzing in her pocket again. She was right on time, so maybe today wouldn't be as bad as she'd thought it would be.

"I think that's my seat." A pale boy with a blond flop of hair over his left eye looked down at Madalyn warily.

"Oh." Madalyn stood up like she'd been poked. "S-Sorry."

"That's okay. Seating chart's up front," he said, gesturing with his chin toward a cluster of students at the whiteboard.

"Thanks." Madalyn took a single step toward the front of the room as the brown-haired woman began to speak. "Seventh graders, if you haven't noticed the seating chart, please pay attention as I call out your names."

Madalyn waited until the teacher got to Thomas, then meekly took her place in the second row on the right side of the room. The desks filled quickly, and Madalyn studied the people around her. A thin, freckled girl with long legs and a bright-red braid gave Madalyn a shy smile on her way to a desk in the front row. On the other side of the room two girls with golden tans and almost identical light brown haircuts stared in Madalyn's direction, whispering. Madalyn turned away. A boy with a rolling backpack and hearing aids took the desk next to Madalyn and pulled out a book. His light brown skin made Madalyn take another glance around the room to confirm. Yep, there were other brown-skinned students, but no one quite like her. She was the only Black girl in this class. Well, that was one thing that was different from Robinson Howard Middle School.

The second thing that was different was that Robinson Howard had had fifteen hundred students. Even at Madalyn's old elementary school in Gold Hill there had been more students than at this school. There were twenty-four seventh-grade students in first-period Language Arts/History block. This period, according to the teacher, Ms. Castaic, was a quarter of the whole seventh grade. Madalyn looked around the room again, blinking. It was weird to think that some people in first period probably knew every single person in the whole seventh grade.

"These will be your seats for our Language Arts/History block the entire semester," Ms. Castaic was saying. "But you won't be using them now. Right now, I want you to stand up, come to the front of the room, and gather in blobs or lines by . . . shoe." Into the bewildered pause that followed, Ms. Castaic smiled and added, "It can be by color or style or size. Find the people in this room who have shoes in common with yours. Go!"

Well, this was certainly the third thing that was different from Robinson Howard Middle School. Madalyn looked down at her sparkly green ballet flats. She'd picked shoes with a little pop of color on purpose, but no one else in the room had green shoes—probably. Madalyn stood up uncertainly and almost bumped into the red-haired girl. They both looked down at their shoes in unison. The girl's shoes were gray ballet flats with cat faces on the toes.

"Those are cute," Madalyn said, shyness making her voice quiet.

"So are yours," the girl said. "I guess we're both wearing flats . . . ?"

"That counts," Madalyn agreed. "And the cats' eyes are green. We're good."

"Whew!"

Within a few minutes, a big, tall girl with a pale, round, freckled face and long brown hair swinging above her hips had joined, pointing wordlessly at her red-and-white-striped flats with an elegantly long fingernail. She curtsied when Wendy, the girl with the red hair, gave her a thumbs-up. A girl with light brown skin, a ponytail, and a shaved undercut had sauntered over in her glittery gold tennis shoes. She had pins all over her denim vest and pointed at Madalyn's sparkly flats.

"I'm Aria, I think we're glitter twins?"

The other girls had looked at each other and

shrugged. "Seems legit," Wendy decided, and they all giggled.

A curly-haired blond girl with green-and-white-striped loafers came and stood next to Natalie, the tall girl with the striped shoes, and claimed her space by way of matching stripes. By the time ten girls had gathered around in a loose blob around Wendy and Madalyn, Madalyn was shaking her head in amusement. None of the shoes in this group exactly *matched*, not really. She wasn't sure this was what Ms. Castaic had planned, but it was all working out. Best of all, her leg hardly hurt anymore at all.

"Okay, shoe groups! Line up in alphabetical order by your first names! Go!"

This was much easier. Names were exchanged and lines were formed—then re-formed, as mix-ups occurred. Alphabetizing with bodies was slightly harder with an Emma and an Emily, a Chloe and a Charlotte. Then Aria did an impressive salsa step toward her spot, and their whole line dissolved into an impromptu dance party. Ms. Castaic just smiled and shook her head at them, her blue eyes twinkling.

"New groups!" was the next instruction. "We're hanging out by seasons. If you were born in summertime like I was, join me here! Spring babies, by the whiteboard! Winters, by the window! Autumns, by the door!" Madalyn waved goodbye to Wendy and headed for the Winter kids by the window. She was joined by the boy with the floppy blond hair, by Natalie Parry, with her Rapunzel hair and stripey shoes, and by the two girls who had been whispering. The one with the wispy bangs looked Madalyn over and smiled. "Cute shoes. From Kiks in the mall?"

"Thanks. My mom got them . . . somewhere." Madalyn shrugged.

"Very cute," the other girl observed, and the two of them examined Madalyn's outfit in silence. Madalyn glanced down, wondering if she had toothpaste on her shirt. She was tempted to do a slow turn and hold out her arms or stick out her tongue. They were staring again.

Ms. Castaic had them moving again. This time, they grouped by how many languages other than English they could speak. Madalyn would have stuck to the one-language group, except that when she'd been small and obsessed with *Dora the Explorer*, she and Daddy had taken a Spanish class together at the community center. Madalyn used a Spanish learning app on her phone ten minutes a day, and could say *No me gusta la sopa de brócoli*, and *¿Dónde está la* *biblioteca?* She knew a bit of Louisiana Creole French, but she wasn't sure that counted, since she didn't actually *know*-know it. Aria convinced Madalyn that her Spanish, at least, counted and dragged Madalyn with her to the two-language group. Ms. Castaic applauded when Aria introduced her in Spanish. Just for fun, Madalyn introduced Aria in Spanish *and* French.

"So, where did you come from?" The pair of girls was at Madalyn's elbow again. Ms. Castaic was having them line up by eye color, and since both of the light-haired girls had brown eyes, they had trailed her across the room to the next big group.

"From Gold Hill," Madalyn answered automatically, forgetting they didn't live there anymore.

"No, I mean . . . where are you *from*-from?" the girl asked again, waving her hand as if that explained more. "Why do you speak Spanish?"

Madalyn frowned and ran her fingers over her braid, remembering all the time she'd spent at Avery's house, learning Puerto Rican Spanish vocabulary from Avery's dad and eating her mom's Trinidadian food. "Uh . . . because? I learned it."

Fortunately, they were all too busy to ask any more questions for a while. Ms. Castaic had the whole room line up by birthday, from January first to December thirty-first. This took up the rest of Ms. Castaic's time and Madalyn forgot their questions once Ms. Furukawa started talking about books. By the time the teacher excused them to go to Math 7, Madalyn was chatting with Wendy and Natalie, and she had mostly forgotten all about the weird questions until Natalie, who was explaining how she'd gotten the little aliens on her fingernails—they were actually from a nail-stamping kit—interrupted herself to mutter, "Oh no."

"What's wrong?" Madalyn looked around. The same two brown-haired girls were pushing through the crowd in Madalyn's direction. "Who are they?" she asked Natalie. "They never told me their names."

"That's Carlin and Sydney," Natalie warned. "Don't look directly at them. If you meet their eyes, I'm pretty sure they get mind control over you or something. Like vampires."

Madalyn blinked at Natalie, then burst out laughing. She was definitely going to be friends with this girl. Avery would *love* Natalie.

"What's funny?" Carlin, or maybe Sydney, intercepted Madalyn next to the water fountain.

"Just something Natalie said." Madalyn smiled, adding, "Do you guys know Natalie?"

"Yeah, hi," the girl said, giving Natalie a brief look.

"Hey, so I wanted to ask you where you got your earrings. You're Addy, like that American Girl doll, right?"

"No, my name is *Madalyn*." Madalyn fingered the mismatched tassels dangling from her ears to remind herself which earrings she was wearing. "And I made my earrings."

"Seriously?" Natalie interrupted. "That's cool. Maybe you can show me how sometime."

"It's easy," promised Madalyn. "It's basically just lots of little knots in embroidery thread. We can bring some thread and do up a pair at lunch."

"Yeah, they're supercute, aren't they, Syd?" Carlin said, walking backward for a second to get in front of Madalyn. She examined Madalyn's face again. "So, you're from Gold Hill? Is that where your parents are from?"

"No," Madalyn said, feeling her forehead wrinkling. Even though her mouth almost opened to supply the answers of exactly where they were from, Madalyn stopped herself. That wasn't anyone's business. She added, uncertainly, "Um . . . why?"

Carlin gave Madalyn a long look, studying her face again. "Well, it's obvious you're not from around here," she said, and shrugged.

Madalyn blinked as Sydney brushed past her, following Carlin to a desk at the back of the room. Madalyn looked at Natalie, who looked . . . at the floor.

In the pause that followed, Madalyn said, half jokingly, "Wow. So, do you think that means she wants to meet my parents?" But even as she smiled, Madalyn rubbed her damp hands against her capris. Carlin had made her feel weird and unwelcome. Why would she do that?

Natalie laughed nervously. "Who knows, right? Vampires. I told you not to look at them too long."

Madalyn shook her head as the mathematics teacher called out, "Let's all find a seat!" Since there was no seating chart, Madalyn sat next to Natalie at a table in the second row. Wendy, who had caught up with them, sat behind Natalie, and Aria was in the front row. The vampires sat across the aisle.

They all smiled at each other. Madalyn smiled too, but her smile was a little faded now. She glanced at the clock, wondering if it was too soon to want the day to be over.

The Wind Rises

"Miss Maddy."

"Madalyn."

"C'mon, *ché*, you waking up in there? Madalyn!"

Madalyn pried her face up from the pillow. The sheer white curtains pulled over the window refracted leaves from the backyard onto the white fabric, filling the bedroom with shifting, yellow-green afternoon shadows, as if the wide bed were underwater. For a moment, Madalyn lay blinking, eyeing the old-fashioned leaf-print paper on the wall closest to her in confusion. "Huh?"

"You decent, *mamzél*?"

Oh. Madalyn remembered where she was and

blinked down at her tank top, adjusting the wedgie her shorts were giving her. It was after school, she had gone into her room to read for a while, and . . . "I'm . . . dressed," Madalyn croaked. She wondered exactly what "decent" was in Papa Lobo's world.

"Jean's come round," Papa Lobo announced, still on the other side of the door.

"Okay." Madalyn waited. When she heard nothing further, Madalyn blurted, "Jean's come to see *me*?" Still nothing.

Madalyn sighed into the silence. "Okay. Coming."

Rubbing her face, Madalyn struggled upright and slipped on a pair of flip-flops. Yawning, she shuffled down the hall into the bright-yellow kitchen. Papa Lobo had just lowered himself into a chair and was reaching for his coffee—probably the same cup he'd been sipping from when Madalyn had gotten home from school an hour ago—and gave her an amused look. His wide grin at her sheet-creased face and pillow-fuzzed braid bunched up in a scowl when he reached her legs.

"You fall off that bike, *mamzél*? Why's your leg all tore up? I need to call Doc to come look at you!"

"Oh." Madalyn looked down at the scabby road rash on her leg. "It wasn't the bike. I tripped."

Papa Lobo glared across the kitchen to where Jean was sitting in cutoffs and a band T-shirt. "Jean Baptiste," he said, accusation in his voice.

"Sir?" Jean looked up from his phone at Papa Lobo's stern voice. Madalyn noticed that he wore the same scuffed black boots.

"*Fiyo*, you were supposed to be watching out for her."

He was? Madalyn frowned. Mom hadn't said anything to her about *that*. "No, he wasn't," she said loudly, interrupting whatever Jean was attempting to say. "Papa Lobo, I'm in the seventh grade. I can watch out for myself. Anyway, I didn't even know Jean went to Kingsbridge."

"'Course he does," Papa Lobo said, and reached into his pocket, ignoring the rest of Madalyn's comment. "You two take your bikes and run on up to the market, get yourselves an ice cream. And bring me back some avocados," he added, handing Jean cash.

Jean took the twenty-dollar bill, stood, and shoved it into his pocket. He jerked his chin at Madalyn. "Let's go," he said, and vanished into the hallway.

Madalyn gave Papa Lobo a startled glance. He'd woken her up from a nap, and now she was just supposed to *go* with some boy who didn't even talk to her?

"Whatcha waitin' on?" Papa Lobo asked, sipping his coffee and giving her a sneaky grin.

Madalyn sputtered and hurried after Jean.

With no time to do more than grab her wallet, Madalyn rubbed the sleep from her eyes and hustled out after Jean, who was sitting astride his bike, looking at his phone. Madalyn clamped her helmet on and wheeled her bike from around the side of the house. She stopped a few feet away. She'd never been to the store by herself with a boy she didn't really know. She wondered how far away the store was, and if Jean really wanted her to go with him. Was this him having to "look out for her" again? She didn't need that!

"Jean?"

"What?" He didn't look up.

Madalyn winced. Whatever she said would sound dumb. "Never mind," she mumbled.

Jean sighed aloud and slipped his phone into his pocket. "*What*, Ma-da-lyn," he enunciated.

Madalyn's eyes narrowed. He sounded just like Avery's brother, Antony, did when Avery asked him for something he didn't want to give. Madalyn did her best to sound like Avery. "*You*, that's what," she snapped back. "I didn't ask you to look out for me, so . . . don't."

49

"You can't stop me." Jean shrugged and pushed off from the curb.

Madalyn opened her mouth, blinked, then closed it again. She hopped on her bike and pedaled after him. "Um, Jean?"

"What?"

"Aren't you going to wear a helmet?"

"Nope."

"You're going to get a ticket," Madalyn warned.

"No, I'm not," Jean said, speeding up.

Madalyn, squinting, sweating, concentrated on keeping pace with Jean's much longer legs. They were going in the exact opposite direction of the school, straight down the whole of Gatland Street, and then up onto the sidewalk, through two metal poles, and onto a bike trail. Madalyn looked around with interest as they pedaled past the backs of apartment and office buildings, and past a park. The hills above the town were a deep, baked gold, with clumps of dark green scrub rippling in the soft wind. Along the trail, the golden-brown weeds were hip high and filled with the dry scrape of cricket and cicada song. It was still hot, but Madalyn started to enjoy the warm wind drying her forehead.

They came off the trail between another two metal

poles, and there was a shopping center, a gas station on the corner, and a couple of fast-food shops.

"Now you know how to get to the store, and *Paren* can make you get his avocados," Jean said, coasting to a stop in front of Fareway Market.

Madalyn's brows raised. "I don't mind," she said. Mom had never asked her to ride her bike to the store in Gold Hill, and she certainly hadn't last school year at the new house.

"You'll mind when it's raining," Jean said, and went inside the blissfully cool air-conditioning.

Madalyn didn't exactly shop *with* Jean. He stalked through the produce department, and she trailed a few feet behind him, looking at things like the weird, bumpy gourds at the front of the store, the caramel wrappers, which were near the apples, and the bouquets of sunflowers in galvanized buckets at the cash register. She almost reached for a bouquet, except Jean shook his head.

"Don't bother with those. Ma has 'em all over the yard, if you want 'em," he said.

"You sure she won't mind if I take some?" Madalyn missed her mother's flowers arranged on the kitchen table.

Jean shook his head and put the bag of avocados on

the counter in front of the gum-chewing older woman who eyed Madalyn with curiosity. "Nope. Be glad of it, probably."

"Your total is $12.63," the woman inserted, tearing off Jean's receipt. She winked a faded blue eye, her gray-streaked braid swinging forward as she bent to smile down at Madalyn. "Who's your little friend, Jean?"

Jean's mouth turned down. "She's not my friend, she's just the neighbor," he announced, holding out the money.

"Be nice, Jean," the woman tsked. She beamed at Madalyn, who was glaring at Jean. "I'm Mrs. Haven. I've been a checker here since this guy was just a little sprout. It's nice to see new faces in the neighborhood."

"Um, thanks." Madalyn smiled politely, resisting the urge to kick Jean in the ankle. Well, he wasn't *her* friend, either.

"You kids have a nice day now," Mrs. Haven said, and handed back Jean's change. He grunted something and hurried out, leaving Madalyn to practically have to run to catch up with him.

Madalyn didn't know what Jean's problem was, but she had a few things to say about her not being his friend. She was just getting ready to say something snarky and sharp when she realized. "Jean! We didn't get ice cream!"

Jean smirked, knotting the avocado bag and dumping it into his backpack. "You don't get it at the market, you get it at the drugstore," he said, jerking his chin at the building next door, as if this explained everything. "What kind do you want?"

Madalyn shrugged. She wasn't supposed to have dairy anymore, but it was hard to pass up a cone at the drugstore. "I like orange sherbet, but—"

"They have rainbow," Jean interrupted. "It's got raspberry, lime, and orange, so that's close enough. I'll get you that, and some brownie bits, okay? One of us has to stay out here, because we can't go in with a backpack, and I don't want to leave the avocados. Two scoops or three?"

Madalyn laughed, her mood improving. "Duh. Three."

"Right," Jean grunted. "Be right back."

Well, all right. He might not be her friend, but . . . brownie bits could make a lot of things better.

Madalyn leaned against her bike and kicked idly at the curb as cars slid in and out of the parking lot. Carts rattled as a yellow-vested girl chased them down and dragged them forcefully back to the grocery store. The plate glass doors to the drugstore opened, and a round pale woman, her dark brown hair piled high, stepped out in a dark blue business dress and red high-heeled shoes. A huge purse was looped around her forearm, and she cradled a single-scoop ice-cream cone in one hand. Her bright-red nails flashed as she gestured with her other hand while talking to the long-haired girl in a T-shirt and cutoffs walking slowly behind her.

"No. No, that's not going to work. I have a meeting at the capitol at two, we'll have to reschedule," the woman said, striding briskly past Madalyn, her heels tapping. Madalyn noticed the white earbud in her ear just before she recognized the girl behind her, carrying a bag from the drugstore and licking a double-scoop cone.

"Natalie!" Madalyn squealed, waving.

Natalie almost levitated off the sidewalk. Her pale cheeks went blotchy, and her eyes went wide as she looked around.

"It's me!" Madalyn waved again, and Natalie stared at her, wide-eyed, then scowling. Suddenly, her expression cleared, and she put a hand to her chest.

"*Oh!* Um, Madalyn. Hi." Natalie smiled weakly.

"Sorry," Madalyn apologized, face hot with embarrassment. "Didn't mean to scare you."

"No, I'm just—" Natalie waved a hand and gulped. "I didn't see you, um, standing there."

Didn't see her? Natalie had stared at her for, like, ten seconds. Maybe it was because they hadn't been at school, and they'd only just met. Maybe she had only seen a Black girl, a stranger and not a friend. Madalyn hesitated, then changed the subject, nodding at the woman who had stopped to watch them a moment before walking across the parking lot. She was still on her phone call. "Is that your mom? You guys look so much alike."

Which was somehow the wrong thing to say. Natalie's face got even blotchier. "No, that's not my mom," she mumbled. "That's my half sister, Annica. We have different dads."

"Oh!" Madalyn said. She noticed how embarrassed Natalie looked and stifled her curiosity. She wouldn't ask where Natalie's parents were. She wouldn't ask how come Natalie was her age, but her sister looked like she was as old as Mom and Daddy. "That's nice. I mean, it seems nice to me, since I don't have any sisters . . . or brothers, either." Madalyn trailed off awkwardly.

"Oh," said Natalie, then licked the side of her cone. "Sorry, it's melting," she apologized.

Madalyn waved a hand, relieved to see Jean coming out of the drugstore at last. "Well, eat it, then. What kind did you get?"

"Nat!"

"Coming!" Natalie waved but didn't jump this time. "One scoop is coffee, and one scoop is vanilla bean," she told Madalyn. "We call it the Iced Latte. Annica invented—"

Just then, Jean walked up and handed Madalyn her sherbet. Natalie's eyes went wide. Her fair skin turned blotchy red again, and she took two jerky steps back.

"One rainbow sherbet," Jean said, then glanced at Natalie with a quick lift of his chin. "What's up?"

Natalie mumbled something and hurried away.

"See you tomorrow?" Madalyn called, but Natalie didn't slow. Madalyn stared after her, bewildered, as Natalie got into the car, head down. She didn't even look back as the car pulled away. Madalyn licked the sherbet from the base of the cone and frowned.

Jean bit off a chunk of ice cream with his teeth and made a happy noise in the back of his throat. "Mmm. You ready?"

"Yeah," Madalyn said slowly, even though she felt unsettled and confused. She licked the softened dessert from around the outside of the scoops and wiped her mouth with the back of her hand. "Hey, Jean?"

"Hmm?"

"Do you know Natalie?"

"Who?" Jean's brows rose, and he took another massive bite of ice cream.

"Never mind," Madalyn muttered.

Shrugging, Jean pedaled away, steering the bike with his knees in a leisurely path across the parking lot. Frowning, Madalyn rode awkwardly after him, one hand on her handlebars, wondering what had just happened.

A Chilly Mist

Chewing on the last bite of toast, Madalyn patted her comforter straight, grabbed her backpack, and hurried toward the front door. After her phone call with Mom last night, they'd both agreed that she needed to be a little better prepared today, so Thursday night she had showered and packed her lunch as usual, but also laid out her clothes and planned out her breakfast. She was nearly out the front door—right on time—when she heard a quick one-two knock and then the turning of a key in the lock.

"*Paren*, where y'at?" Jean hollered, opening the door. "I— Hey, Madalyn."

"What are you doing—oh!" Madalyn went from

suspicion to delight in a heartbeat as she made grabby hands toward Jean's backpack. "You brought them!"

Jean yanked out the bundle of pale gold sunflowers he'd shoved down a side pocket in his pack and thrust them toward her. "Yeah. Mama says you can come by and cut whatever you want."

"Ooh, tell her thank you!" Madalyn hurried back toward the kitchen, fluffing some squashed petals. These were the prettiest sunflowers she'd ever seen. "Papa Lobo's in the backyard reading the paper."

"Uh-huh." Jean leaned against the dark wood counter and watched as Madalyn took a plastic pitcher from the drainer and created a hasty temporary vase. She looked at the clock on the stove and winced. She hadn't wanted to hurry this morning—her leg was still hurting—and if she didn't want to rush, she had to go *right now.*

"Bye," Madalyn called, and hurried back down the hall.

Jean followed, locking the door behind them before she could get out her key.

Madalyn scowled. Jean was going in the same direction as she was, but she didn't need him locking the door behind her.

Madalyn wheeled her bike out from around the side

of the house and buckled on her helmet.

Jean sat on his bike at the end of the driveway, eyes on his phone.

Madalyn narrowed her eyes. "Are you waiting for me?"

Jean didn't look up. "Nope."

Slowly, Madalyn pushed off from the curb and pedaled up the street. When she glanced behind her, Jean was keeping pace, a few feet away.

Scowling, Madalyn slowed.

When she glared over her shoulder the next time, Jean was still the same distance away.

Somehow, every time she turned around, Jean wasn't any closer or any farther away. Madalyn sped up. And slowed way, way down. And sped up again. Jean was still there—and she couldn't shake him! He wouldn't pass her, he wouldn't catch up, he was just . . . there, keeping an eye on her, just like Papa Lobo wanted.

Madalyn couldn't decide if that was sweet or annoying.

By the time she got to school, Madalyn was riding even faster than she had the first day when she thought she was late. Her leg was throbbing, and she just *barely* made the turn into the narrow path between the fences that was just for bikes and jerked to a stop by the first bike rack, preparing to give Jean Duval a piece of her mind about following her, no matter what Papa Lobo had said. She twisted, mouth open, and—

He wasn't there.

Shaken, Madalyn looked around. Jean had skipped the bike lane and turned in at the broad driveway to the school that cars used. Now he was standing, balanced on his pedals, talking to someone . . . and someone else was waving. At her.

"Wendy! Aria!" Madalyn beamed, locking up her bike, Jean and his annoyingness forgotten for the moment. She and Mom had talked last night about how to handle the girls at school, and Madalyn was relieved not to see Carlin and Sydney anywhere. It was nice to be met by smiling faces on only her second day.

"Hey, you look nice," Aria said, examining Madalyn's gauzy blue top with the swoopy embroidered sleeves. "That looks like it's from Mexico."

"It's from El Salvador," Madalyn said. "My mom's auntie Della went on an artist tour and brought me back a shirt."

"Cool," Aria said, a little enviously.

Madalyn smiled, feeling her mood lift like fog burning away to show off the sunshine. She hiked her backpack up on her shoulder and moved closer to Wendy, who had hung back a little behind Aria. "Hey, Wendy," Madalyn said, including the taller girl in the conversation, "I like your hair up like that."

"Thanks," Wendy said, fingering her Princess Leia buns. "Um, Madalyn, I need to tell you something. Natalie called me yesterday . . ."

Aria sighed loudly, and Wendy winced.

"What? I saw her after school and . . . is she mad at me?" Madalyn swallowed hard and looked from Wendy to Aria. "What did I do?"

Aria sighed again. "Look. Don't—I don't think Nat's right about this. So, don't, um . . . don't get mad, okay?"

Madalyn's eyes widened. She *knew* something had made Natalie act so weird. "Did I do something wrong? She was acting weird—"

"No, no, no," Wendy interrupted, waving her hands. "Okay, look. Natalie really likes you, but last year at Pleasant Grove, Natalie got bullied by this one kid, and it got *really* bad. He was really funny, right? Like, he and his friends made everything sound like they were kidding. They made fun of teachers, and kind of did joke insult battles and stuff—you know? I actually thought he was someone Natalie talked to—he was around a lot. But she *didn't* talk to him, and he would, like, walk by and trash her backpack all the time."

Madalyn's scowl was like thunderclouds. "Jerk."

"It wasn't even just that," Aria added. "He would say mean things to her when she was by herself, and flick spit balls in her hair, and make fun of her weight and the way she walks. I think teachers thought he liked her because he was always around her."

"That's *unacceptable*," Madalyn said, using one of Mom's favorite angry words. "I hate it when people say stupid stuff like that. Why would he be mean to Natalie if he *liked* her?"

"I *know*. It's so dumb," Aria said. "I don't really know Natalie very well, so I didn't know she was sad. I thought she was just really quiet."

"And she never told anyone," Wendy said miserably. "I guess her older sister found out when she noticed Natalie was pulling out her hair or something."

"Oh no!" Madalyn said, horrified.

Wendy nodded, her expression solemn. "She went to pick her up from school, and she saw this guy following her, throwing stuff at her. Annica got the vice principal on the phone, and we had a big old assembly. I felt really bad about it when I found out it was about

Natalie—she didn't even tell me she was the one who was bullied until a month ago. When she saw you at the store with that guy, even though she wants to be friends, she kind of freaked out."

Madalyn opened her mouth. "Wait—" she blurted, and then her phone buzzed. At the same time, Wendy's chimed, and Aria's let out a rooster crow, which made Madalyn smile a little and think of Papa Lobo.

"Five minutes," Aria said, and all three girls began walking, following the surge of students toward classrooms.

"Okay, wait, though," Madalyn said again, turning so she was walking backward in front of the other two. "What does our neighbor Jean have to do with that bullying guy? He wasn't at your old school last year, was he?"

Aria shrugged. "I don't know."

Madalyn felt an odd twisting in her stomach. "What was the bully guy's name?"

"Marc something?" Aria looked questioningly at Wendy, who frowned, shaking her head.

"Matt."

"It was Marc."

Wendy looked exasperated. "It was *Matt*. Aria, Natalie told me, so I should *know*."

"And that's why this is so dumb," Aria said, rolling her eyes at Wendy. "Wendy doesn't even know if the guy's name was Marc or Matt, just like Natalie doesn't know who the guy is you were talking to, but she doesn't like him, and so she was weird with you, because he reminds her of that guy."

"He does?" Madalyn asked. Something wasn't right here. Dread made Madalyn have to force out the word. "How?"

Aria looked at Wendy, who looked away.

"He's Black," Aria said, when Wendy didn't answer.

Madalyn swallowed. For a minute, she couldn't say anything.

What was there *to* say?

"Lame, I know," Aria mumbled, giving Madalyn a look as she went into the classroom. "Sorry."

Wendy's wide mouth turned down unhappily. She glanced at Madalyn, then shrugged apologetically. "Yeah, sorry. I just . . . I wanted to tell you in case . . . Um, I just wanted you to know," she finished awkwardly.

"Thanks, I guess," Madalyn said.

Madalyn had a weird feeling rattling through her, like a tiny earthquake, vibrating.

She was Black, too.

And when Natalie had first seen her at the store, she'd been scared then, too.

Madalyn thought about that all through Ms. Castaic's good morning, and her reintroducing Ms. Furukawa, who taught the Language Arts part of the block. Madalyn kind of zoned out as Ms. Castaic talked about history and the movement of tribes and groups—or blobs of people by shoe colors—and what that had to do with the Romans. She couldn't be sure she actually understood any of the reasons Ms. Castaic gave for the fall of the Roman Empire, but she carefully wrote down that it happened and listed all the reasons given on the whiteboard.

She didn't look out the window when a whistle blew and eighth graders in baseball uniforms ran by in groups, jogging around the yellowed grass on the baseball diamond. Madalyn was thinking so hard she didn't even notice Wally, the boy in the assigned seat next to hers, slide his foot into the aisle until the note hit her shoe.

Startled, Madalyn did a fake-accidental pencil drop and swiped the paper between her fingers. She unfolded the note behind her history book.

Your shirt's Mexican, right? —Carlin

Madalyn blinked, then wanted to laugh. She'd forgotten all about the vampire girls who had stared at her,
whispering, and now that she remembered, Madalyn
felt scornful. Carlin and Sydney had worried Madalyn
so much that she'd talked to Mom about them. She'd
told Mom that the way they'd talked to her had made
her feel jumpy and angry for most of the day. Mom had
told Madalyn what she always did. "Just walk in there
being your own brilliant self and see what happens. You
don't have to be a reflection of anyone else's attitude—
be your own original work of art."

Madalyn had been thinking so hard about Natalie,
she'd forgotten to even worry about Carlin's and Sydney's attitudes toward her. Now, looking vampire
Carlin in the eyes didn't seem nearly as bad as having to look at Natalie sitting right next to her next
period. Carlin was just nosy and rude. What was
Madalyn going to say to someone who had been so
nice, who maybe thought she was a bad person for
hanging around with Jean, or whatever it was Natalie
was thinking?

Madalyn wadded up the note and shoved it into
the pocket of her binder without bothering to answer.
Madalyn hated bullies. She hated how bad Natalie's
experience had made her feel, and how much it had

scared her. Madalyn wanted to be on Natalie's side, because Natalie was a new friend, and she'd been hurt by a mean boy, but Madalyn was sure Natalie wasn't being fair. Was Natalie really wrong for just trying to protect herself against that kind of boy again?

But the other side of Madalyn's brain piped up: What kind of boy was Natalie afraid of?

It wasn't all boys, or just ninth-grade boys, or even only boys who thought they were funny and were really bullies. If she could believe what Wendy and Aria said, it was Black boys, and that made Madalyn's stomach hurt. A lot of people were afraid of Black boys, and Mom said that's why so many of them died—for wearing a hoodie someone thought was scary, or playing with a toy that looked scary, or for just being someone out walking or jogging or living life, who might turn out to be someone scary. Mom said sometimes people made the mistake of killing things they were afraid of, like spiders. Spiders, even though Madalyn really didn't like them, didn't deserve to be squashed just because someone decided they were creepy.

Jean hadn't done anything but eat his ice cream and ride his bike. Madalyn wished that Natalie knew that Jean wasn't even a little bit scary.

Low Pressure Trough

Madalyn pulled out her water bottle and a new note-book for the Language Arts portion of their morning block. Ms. Furukawa, who was a compact, energetic Japanese American lady with a green stripe dyed into her thick dark hair, had picked up their vocabulary warm-up and was writing a free-write prompt on the whiteboard while everyone took a two-minute stretch. Everyone walked away from their desks to stretch but Madalyn. Aria and Wendy got up to chat, and from the corner of her eye, Madalyn could see Natalie talking with them, her long dark hair moving as she waved her hands. Madalyn decided to stay in her seat.

As she sipped her water, Madalyn noticed Sydney

hurrying across the room toward her, Carlin following like her shadow. Madalyn sighed and felt her shoulders slump. She was feeling grumpy and prickly—or grinchly, like Avery called it when she was feeling sour. Madalyn was not in the mood for more of Carlin's nosy questions.

"Hey, that's indigo dye, right?" Sydney said, pointing at the blue of Madalyn's shirt.

"Yeah." Madalyn set down her water bottle and blinked. "How'd you know?"

"I watched a show about indigo farms." Sydney turned to Carlin. "See? Told you."

Carlin rolled her eyes. "Syd's mom is a fabric artist, so she thinks she knows everything."

"That sounds cool," Madalyn said to Sydney. She had no idea what fabric artists did, but she couldn't help taking a closer look at Sydney. Maybe she was more interesting than she'd seemed? "She makes art out of . . . cloth?"

"Thirty seconds," Ms. Furukawa announced. "Let's settle in, please."

"Yep—felt sculptures and jewelry and paintings. And regular quilts and stuff, too."

"Oh," Madalyn said, and then Ms. Furukawa looked at them and said, "Folks?" so Sydney wiggled her fingers and hurried off. Carlin gave Madalyn's top another look before ambling over to her side of the classroom.

Madalyn put her water bottle back in her bag and looked up at the board. The sentence Ms. Furukawa had written was *That was a little unexpected!* Madalyn snickered. It *had* been. The vampires had spoken to her, and they hadn't even tried to take her blood.

A moment later, Ms. Furukawa was at the front of the room, leaning against the table she used as a desk. "Everyone, this morning we're going to do some narrative free writing. A narrative is a story. So, you will be telling your audience a story that has a beginning, a middle, and an end, and uses specific details, like all stories do. Since this is your first draft, spelling does *not* count, but please make sure I can read what you meant to write. When time's up, I'll invite those who would like to, to read them aloud, and for those of you who prefer not to, that's fine; you can turn in your notebooks and only I will read them.

"Back row, this isn't a time for talking. Notebooks out and pencils sharp, everyone. Pens are fine. Ready? Share a time when something unexpected happened to you, or to someone you know. You have fifteen minutes—go!"

Madalyn wrote her name, with her middle initial, in perfect cursive swoops. *Madalyn J. Thomas*. Then she wrote the writing prompt at the top of her blank notebook page and rested the tip of her pencil on the next line. She was not going to be one of the people who wanted to read her work aloud; she had no idea what to write.

Madalyn gnawed her lip and resisted the urge to doodle. Something unexpected . . . unexpected . . . hmmm.

Madalyn looked over and realized she had drawn a spiral that reminded her a lot of the tail of one of Papa Lobo's "cockerels." Then she thought about the coffee she'd watched Papa Lobo make that morning, and suddenly she found herself grinning. Madalyn bent over her notebook, and the words tumbled out in a hasty scrawl.

Papa Lobo had put five scoops of coffee grounds in his little coffee maker, and a scoop of chicory—just like Daddy did—and then, winking at Madalyn, he had added a big pinch of . . . *salt*.

"What are you doing?" she'd blurted, and he'd laughed his scratchy old man laugh and slapped his side.

"Makin' coffee, *ché*," he'd said, and laughed some more.

"What*ever!*" Madalyn said, scowling. She felt special and loved when Papa Lobo called her the Creole word *ché*, like Daddy did, because it meant dear or sweetie, like *ma chérie*. What she didn't like was Papa Lobo laughing at her. He did it a lot because he said Madalyn "tickled him."

"Now, *mamzèl*, don't you go pokin' out your mouth," Papa Lobo told Madalyn, grinning. "I am making coffee. I was in the navy, you know, and there was seawater in everything!" Madalyn smiled a little at the way he said it *ev-rah-ting*. "I drank that coffee for so long, now without a little seawater in it, it don't taste right!"

Madalyn was pretty sure he was making that up—seawater on navy ships *couldn't* get into everything, or else none of the lights or the instruments would work, which were kind of important. If a ship were really that wet, everyone would be cold, and their clothes would be all crunchy, like Madalyn's towel got after a day at the beach. But . . .

Madalyn paused, then started writing again. Ms. Furukawa didn't say Madalyn had to write down if the unexpected thing was *true* or not—just unexpected. Madalyn wrote a bit faster.

Coffee all by itself was kind of unexpected, when

she thought about it—Madalyn remembered the first time Daddy had let her have a tiny sip of his. It had smelled so, so good, but it tasted . . . a *lot* like ink did when she forgot and chewed on a pen lid. Why was it so bitter? Who was the first person who'd decided to drink it? How did people even know that coffee beans growing on a tree were supposed to be edible— or drinkable? She supposed indigenous people were the first ones, but what made *them* think those beans would be good? Did they also drink coffee with sugar? Would they have liked it with salt?

"Time," Ms. Furukawa said from right near Madalyn's shoulder, and Madalyn jumped. She had filled up three pages without stopping, not even noticing that Ms. Furukawa was walking around the room.

"Would anyone like to share what they've written?"

Madalyn was surprised so many people raised their hands. Did Ms. Furukawa give extra credit to people who read or something? She turned as the boy the next seat over from her, Wally, read a funny and sort of gross story about his grandpa always leaving his false teeth in a glass and how he never drinks out of anyone's glass but his own anymore.

The boy with the floppy bangs—Eli? Ian?—read his story about being excited to learn a song called

"Surprise Symphony" in his violin lessons and being disappointed because the surprise didn't really work on him. He admitted that the audience was a little surprised a month later when he played it with the whole orchestra, though.

"Natalie?" Ms. Furukawa said, and Madalyn found her shoulders hunching.

She had very carefully avoided looking at or thinking about Natalie all morning long. Madalyn just wasn't . . . ready for Natalie yet. She wasn't ready to talk to her, or look at her—what if she was looking back? It was too much, and Madalyn didn't want to be rushed to say something before she knew what to say.

And now Natalie was reading.

"Something unexpected happened last year in sixth grade," Natalie began, her voice soft. "A boy I didn't know walked by me talking every day, but at first, I didn't know he was talking to me. I got it when I heard the rude and mean things he was saying. He made fun of my face, my weight, my hair, and everything about me. He told me nobody really liked me."

Natalie paused. Madalyn pressed her hand to her heart where an awful, fluttery sensation made her feel like she couldn't breathe. Even though she already knew a little of this story, there was something so terrible about hearing Natalie read it herself, quietly and calmly, as if each word wasn't a great big hurt that had happened to her every day. Around the room, other people were staring, and Carlin and Sydney were, as usual, whispering. Ms. Furukawa had set down her notebook and was leaning against her desk, watching Natalie with a slight frown on her face.

"I guess bullies aren't all that unexpected, but what I didn't expect is that bullying lasts a long time. Even when the bully stops bothering you. Even when the whole school year is over, and they're not even at your next school. Even when you don't have to worry about seeing them anymore in the same city, it is easy to get scared. I didn't expect that. I thought it was over." Natalie turned around and looked at Ms. Furukawa. "That's all," she said.

"Thank you, Natalie," Ms. Furukawa said, moving to stand up straighter. "A big thank-you to all our brave readers this morning. If everyone would pass up your journals to the front, I'll return them to you tomorrow at the beginning of class. Does anyone know why we freewrite at the beginning of class?"

Around her, people were raising their hands and talking as Ms. Furukawa wrote their thoughts on the board. Madalyn still sat with her shoulders hunched. She wondered why Natalie chose to write about the bully today. At least now she understood a little bit why Natalie had been so weird yesterday, but did it change things? Jean was still not Matt or Marc, or anyone else—he was Jean. Madalyn knew she'd say something to Natalie Math block—she couldn't not talk to her after that, not when they'd be sitting right next to each other.

Ms. Furukawa was setting up for a vocabulary game, so Madalyn tried to pay more attention. By the time the Language Arts/History block was over, she had the beginnings of a plan. She'd leave class before everyone else and stand in the hallway so she could catch Natalie before math. They could talk things out right there, and then finish up at lunch.

"Thank you, everyone, that's all the time we have today," Ms. Furukawa was saying, and immediately people began getting up and grabbing their things. The teacher continued, raising her voice.

"Start thinking of a topic for your persuasive paragraph. Tomorrow, we'll read aloud the first chapter of our novel, so make sure you arrive prepared with your book, please—I don't want to see a bunch of people racing back out to their lockers after class has begun. Natalie, will you stay behind for a moment, please? Thank you."

Madalyn, who by then had grabbed her things and taken three big steps toward Natalie's desk, stopped in the middle of the aisle and grimaced—and then winced as two people almost collided with her.

"Sorry," she muttered, stepping out of the way as Ian—no, *Ethan*—went one way, and Wally went the other. Of course, Ms. Furukawa wanted Natalie to stay behind.

Aria, standing on the other side of Madalyn's desk, tapped her shoulder. "Hey. You going to talk to Natalie now?"

"I *was*," Madalyn said in a low voice, glancing toward the front of the room. Natalie was listening to something the teacher was saying, but she looked uncomfortable. Ms. Furukawa looked up, and then waved.

"Don't be late, folks."

Madalyn could take a hint. "I guess not," she muttered as she, Aria, and Wendy trudged out of the room and into the hall.

"Maybe you could write her a note?" Wendy asked.

"Maybe," Madalyn said, and shrugged, feeling

knotted up with frustration. "It's okay. I didn't know what I was going to say anyway."

The trio walked into Mrs. Solazzo's classroom in glum silence and shuffled to their spots; Aria at the table in front of Madalyn, and Wendy right behind Madalyn. Mrs. Solazzo, who had straight, graying light brown hair and laugh wrinkles around her pale blue eyes, was wearing a yellow-and-brown-striped dress, black tights, and chunky black clogs. Madalyn immediately wished she could loan Mrs. Solazzo her black ladybug antennae headband she'd worn to a costume party two years ago. It would go with that outfit *perfectly*.

The class began, and Mrs. Solazzo began to talk about proportions. Madalyn shifted her elbow as Wendy, from the row behind, tucked a piece of paper beneath her arm.

Do you think she dressed like a bee on purpose?

Madalyn felt giggles rising out of nowhere and covered her laughter with a sudden bout of coughing. Now she couldn't help but imagine Mrs. Solazzo with a small pair of wings on her back. Maybe the math teacher was working on her Halloween costume early.

Just then, in a swoosh of swinging hair, Natalie strode up the aisle. Madalyn's smile drained away as Natalie laid her pass on Mrs. Solazzo's desk and then slid into the seat next to hers.

Now what?

Madalyn concentrated on looking very interested in the imaginary carpet salesmen Mrs. Solazzo was talking about. Now Natalie was here, and Madalyn still didn't know how she was supposed to act. She wished she'd thought faster. Now, especially after Natalie had read her writing assignment out loud, Madalyn felt so many different feelings that she didn't know how to say any of them.

But saying *nothing* might make Natalie think she was mad at her . . . and she wasn't.

Madalyn quietly turned a page in her notebook and zipped out a clean page.

> Hi, Natalie, you're a really good writer.
> I like your nails today.
> ☺ Madalyn

It wasn't everything she wanted to say, but it was something true. Avery always said that if you couldn't say anything nice, you should at least say something true in the nicest way possible, and Madalyn really did like Natalie's nail polish. Today it was a bright blue color, with lighter blue circles scattered over all five fingers. Natalie had a sticker of a tiny fish on her left thumb, and probably another one on her right thumb, but Madalyn couldn't see, because Natalie had out a piece of paper and she was writing as fast as she could.

Madalyn glanced up at the board, wondering if Mrs. Solazzo had given them an assignment yet, but no. Natalie was sliding a piece of paper across the table.

Madalyn swallowed. She almost didn't want to read it. If Natalie said something about Jean, what would Madalyn say back? Could you prove that someone was an okay person just with words?

Do you think Mrs. Solazzo knows she looks like a bee?

Madalyn's lips twitched, and her shoulders dropped with relief. Thank goodness for Mrs. Solazzo. Madalyn wasn't even a little bit disappointed that Natalie hadn't said anything about yesterday. They could talk about it later—at lunch, maybe. When Madalyn was ready, she knew she would know exactly what to say. Later.

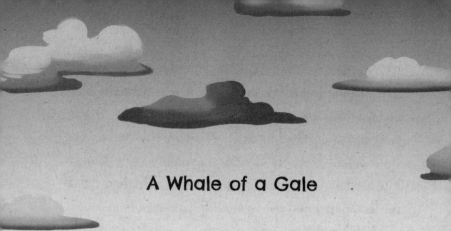

A Whale of a Gale

The quiet knock barely disturbed Madalyn's concentration as she pondered Mrs. Solazzo's first-Friday-of-the-school-year pop quiz. Outside the wind was blowing, as it had all night long, leaving Madalyn with a slightly stuffy nose from her allergies and a sincere wish that she were still in bed.

On the block schedule, Mrs. Solazzo's math classes seemed really short—only forty-five minutes instead of the two-hour-and-twenty-minute block of Language Arts and History with Ms. Furukawa and Ms. Castaic. In math class, it felt like everything went by too fast. Madalyn, who hadn't been paying that much attention on Thursday, due to Mrs. Solazzo's bee outfit, was grateful for the few notes she'd taken and the explanation she'd read in her textbook. She'd read over the quiz instructions twice before realizing Mrs. Solazzo didn't want the answer, just for her to work out how to lay out the problem based on the questions. Once she'd understood, Madalyn had made quick work of the quiz and was pondering the last question.

If it cost $26.58 to fill a six-gallon gas tank with premium unleaded gas, how much would it cost to fill an eighteen-gallon tank? How much did gas cost per gallon? Was it really so expensive? No wonder Mom always complained.

Madalyn's pencil skittered across the paper as Natalie nudged her in the ribs. Madalyn blinked, finally noticing the While You Were Out sticky note Mrs. Solazzo had attached to her textbook.

Madalyn scanned the note quickly—then crumpled it, frowning. Why did Mom want her to call? Madalyn clutched her pencil while worrying at her thumbnail with her teeth. She'd talked to Mom last night as she had every night this week. Mom had talked to Daddy, who was staying in his apartment in Cambridge instead of making the six-hour flight from Massachusetts to California for the weekend. Maybe there'd been a change of plans. Or no, maybe something had *happened* to Daddy. Because Mom *never* interrupted classes.

"What's the matter?" Natalie whispered.

Madalyn whispered, "Nothing," even though her thoughts darted and fluttered like a panicked hummingbird. She wanted to leap up and call Mrs. Solazzo back. She needed a hall pass to get her phone out of her locker, right this second. Lunch was ten minutes away, and there was no way she could wait. But there was still the math quiz, and Mrs. Solazzo standing placidly in the front of the room, asking everyone to pass their paper to the person on their right.

Madalyn sighed and did as she was told.

Ten minutes later, Madalyn was speed walking to the front office. Kingsbridge Junior High cell phone rules said that phones had to be powered down by the first bell, stored in lockers or backpacks, and not turned back on again until the final bell at 3:03 p.m. Students couldn't even call their parents on their cell phones unless they were in the Main Office with permission from the vice principal's office. Madalyn had to show her (uncrumpled) note and her powered-down phone to the school secretary before she was allowed to power up her phone and press the tiny phone icon next to her mother's name. And then she almost wished she hadn't.

"Not until Sunday?" Madalyn knew that she was whining but couldn't stop herself. "I have to stay here all weekend? By myself?"

"I'm sorry, babe, but the office is down three ombudsmen, so we're in emergency mode," Mom said, her voice sounding a bit distracted. Madalyn could hear other voices and the clicks and thumps of the busy people working in her mother's office. "Since your dad isn't flying home this weekend, and I was just there on Wednesday when school started, I thought I could come up on Sunday, spend the night, and leave early Monday morning—so we can both rest up for the week but still spend time together."

"But what am I supposed to *do*?" Madalyn complained.

"Do? What do you usually do on the weekend?" Mom asked.

"Nothing," Madalyn muttered unhappily.

Mom tsked. Madalyn could hear her quick keystrokes as she typed while talking. "Nothing, schmuthing. You go to the library, you make burritos, you watch movies, you and your dad argue about TV shows, you bake something—that's what you usually do. That's not nothing."

"But I can't do all of that with Papa Lobo," Madalyn pointed out.

"Why not?" Mom asked.

Madalyn, who didn't have a good answer, complained, "Well, why didn't you tell me this last night? When you called in the middle of class, I thought something had happened to Daddy!"

"I'm sorry about that, Madalyn. I called as soon as I found out. We're onboarding a new county this month, and—never mind. Look, go to the library and pick out a fun book to read after school. Try out a new recipe and bake your Papa Lobo something. Decorate that nice big room you've got there, maybe borrow some roosters. It'll be Sunday before you know it, Madalyn."

"Ugh. Mom—" Madalyn began.

"I know you don't like it, babe. *I* don't like it, either. But it is what it is."

Madalyn heaved a huge sigh and glowered at a square of the beige-and-blue carpet beneath her feet. "It is what it is" meant that Mom was finished discussing things, and anything else Madalyn said would be starting an argument. Madalyn hated arguing; she almost never did it, because when she argued, she lost her temper. When she lost her temper, Madalyn almost always cried. She didn't want to cry at school, or worse, in front of the school secretary, who was watching her, even though she was mostly pretending to type on her computer.

Madalyn blew out another big sigh. "Fine, *bye*," she said, her voice sharper than she intended. "I have to eat."

"I miss you, too, babe," her mother replied, which Madalyn already knew, but she didn't think that was exactly the point just now.

Moodily poking the power button on her phone, Madalyn waved the blank screen at the hovering secretary and slouched her way out of the front office. Not even Natalie waiting for her at her locker lifted Madalyn's sour mood. Not even the crunchy gingersnaps Papa Lobo had left out for Madalyn's lunch sweetened her up. She was glad her first class after lunch on Fridays was PE, and she was especially glad they were going to start playing soccer, since she was very much in the mood for kicking things.

"You should come over." Aria invited her as they walked to the bike racks after school. "My abuela's here, but she always comes over, so you can still visit, too."

"Thanks, but I should probably spend time with my

uncle," Madalyn said politely. She liked Aria, but she felt too cranky and out of sorts to be anywhere but home—and if she couldn't *really* be home, with Mom and Daddy, then she at least wanted to be in her new bedroom with all her books and things. "I want to get all my homework done before Sunday, too."

"You're as bad as Wendy," Aria groaned. "*She* goes to the library on Friday afternoon to work. *I* leave my homework till Sunday night like a *normal* person."

Wendy, who was putting on her bike helmet nearby, stuck out her tongue.

Aria chortled. "I'm just kidding. Call me if you get bored, Madalyn," she added, and strapped on her own helmet.

"I will," Madalyn said, and waved as Wendy and Aria pedaled away. Madalyn felt a little better as she pedaled off in the opposite direction. She didn't know Aria very well, but like Avery, she was the kind of person who was exactly the same all the time. Maybe Madalyn would run into Wendy at the library later— that might be fun.

There were plenty of kids walking and riding home, in groups and singly. A cluster of boys going in the opposite direction briefly surrounded Madalyn, talking—well, shouting, really—about some game, before they scattered down the road. A delivery truck rattled around the corner and accelerated.

Madalyn stood up on her pedals as she made the turn down Gatland Street. The tree-lined road was quiet as the neighborhood baked under the late-afternoon sun. There wasn't any hurry, really, to get to Papa Lobo's house—except if she wanted to hurry and put on a pair of shorts. It was still hot in September, and Madalyn was sweating away from the air-conditioned classroom. Sighing, she executed a perfect figure eight at the end of Gatland and headed toward the line of evergreen bushes that edged the sidewalk in front of Papa Lobo's house. Home, sweet (for now) home.

Madalyn had just hopped off her bike to open the side gate when she heard a clang and an angry chittering. She twisted, looking up at the tree across the street. A gray cat shot off like a streak up the sidewalk and practically leapt up the smooth bark. From above, the chittering only grew louder. Madalyn saw a brown squirrel running along a telephone wire. It stopped and scolded furiously toward the tree, then ran a little farther away.

Madalyn looked in the direction the cat had come from and was surprised to see a thin figure, her pale face nearly hidden by a wide straw hat, peering at her from across a high fence. The woman vanished for a moment, then reappeared as the gate to her yard opened and she clumped out in her rubber gardening boots. She bent to pick up a trowel from the sidewalk and tucked it into a pocket of the brown apron she wore, scowling up at the telephone wire. Madalyn smiled. With her big straw hat, boots, and apron, the lady looked like the Little Red Hen doll Madalyn had when she was five.

"Terrible, arrogant creature," the woman muttered, then turned to Madalyn. "Good afternoon, dear. Was that your cat?" Her surprisingly deep voice carried across the road with precise syllables.

"Um, no, ma'am, not mine," Madalyn said, brows raised. She didn't think Papa Lobo had a cat, either, but she was too intimidated to say so—she guessed the lady had *thrown* her trowel at the cat; that's what the noisy clatter had been.

The woman placed a hand on her narrow chest and exhaled dramatically. "Oh, *good*. I know I shouldn't have *thrown* anything, but stray cats are a gardener's worst enemy. Always slinking around, digging, spraying; always burying their nasty business all over—and killing my songbirds. House cats belong in the *house*," the lady ranted, and pushed off her hat. Her hair was a striking pure white against her pale freckled skin, which was as softly wrinkled as crumpled silk. Her fine-boned face held a disapproving expression as she continued. "That Mr. Thomas feeds the strays and then they come and dig in my garden. It was bad enough that rascal fed squirrels—squirrels, when they're nothing but common rats!"

"Um . . . ?" Madalyn was completely baffled. They'd gone from cats to rats?

The woman gave a slight cough and waved a hand. "Never mind, my dear. Ignore an old woman's fussing." She gave Madalyn a small smile. "I hadn't realized Mr. Thomas had such a lovely granddaughter."

"Oh, I'm not his granddaughter," Madalyn said, feeling a tiny bit pleased to be called lovely in the middle of the strange conversation. "Papa Lobo's my great-uncle. I'm Madalyn."

"I am so pleased to meet you, Madalyn. I am Mrs. John Baylor," the woman said, giving an elegant nod like some kind of royalty. "I look forward to seeing you around the neighborhood." She smiled and turned back to her yard, then paused, lifting an admonishing finger. "But please, dear—do tell your great-uncle to *Stop*. Feeding. That. Cat." She bit off each word fiercely, and Madalyn's eyes widened.

"I—yes, ma'am." Madalyn gulped.

"That's a good girl. You have a pleasant afternoon, now." Mrs. Baylor beamed, sweetness restored, and turned away, boots clomping hollowly against the sidewalk. Her gate clattered behind her, and all Madalyn could see of her was the straw of her hat bobbing beneath the gate arch, before it was lost among the green plants.

Madalyn paused a moment, in case—well, in case *something*. Talking to Mrs. Baylor was kind of like being in a play. She had a way of speaking that enunciated all the words, as if an audience were listening. And the words she used! Madalyn would always think of squirrels now as "terrible, arrogant creatures."

Madalyn peered across at the woman's yard. It *was* nice—much nicer than Papa Lobo's white quartz stones and dusty laurel bushes. Skinny rose trees with perfectly round spheres of greenery splashed with yellow roses edged a narrow walkway to the front door. The top of a stacked-up fountain poked above the garden fence, trickling enticingly clear water from a small bowl at the top. There were lines of flowers—some tall and pretty—and some kind of flowering vines in baskets hanging along the front porch. Madalyn couldn't see much beyond that, because the fence after the gate was taller, and the plants made a dense second wall beyond it.

Madalyn blinked and opened the side gate to Papa Lobo's house, pushing her bike through. Well, at least she could tell Mom *something* had happened this first weekend alone—she'd met the neighbor lady who disapproved of cats and wasn't all that approving of Papa Lobo, either.

Madalyn glanced back in time to see the gray cat casually leap from the tree to land lightly on the fence. It stretched its back, tail curling around itself, as if nothing had happened.

Madalyn grinned. Mrs. Baylor would probably call the cat arrogant, too. "Hey, kitty," she said softly. "Maybe you'd better stay over on *this* side of the street for a while."

The cat meowed and hopped down from the fence to rub itself against Madalyn's ankle. Madalyn darted a quick, guilty glance across the street, then bent down and stroked a hand up the friendly feline's back. "Be good. Leave the birds alone," she whispered in its pointed ear, then wheeled her bike into the backyard.

Lazy Winds

"I'm back!" Madalyn yelled, bounding through the back door into the kitchen. Papa Lobo was usually right there in his recliner with a cup of coffee, but today she didn't see him. She waited a moment, walking slowly down the hallway. "Papa Lobo?"

"Ey, *mamzèl*, that you?" Papa Lobo's voice came from deep within the house. Madalyn followed the small thuds and a strange, sweetish sharp smell to discover Papa Lobo far on the other end of the house, in the company room. He'd pushed the furniture away from the walls and was squatting in the back corner of the room, behind the biggest couch. Above his head, the artificial forest wallpaper looked dark and slightly wrinkled.

"Papa Lobo," Madalyn said, slinging her backpack across the plastic-covered loveseat nearest the door, "do we have a cat?"

"A cat?" Papa Lobo straightened, shoving a metal tool into his pocket and wiping his hands down the front of his coverall. "You seen a cat in this house?"

Madalyn felt silly. "Well, no, but . . . Mrs. John Baylor, the neighbor, asked if we had one. I was just making sure."

Papa Lobo scowled, his eyes narrowing. "Hmph. I'll just bet she did."

Madalyn didn't know what to make of that. "She said something about not feeding it."

Papa Lobo grunted and turned back to the wall, pulling out his tool again. "*That* woman! Gets on my *last* nerve sometimes." Papa Lobo scraped something against the wall, raising his voice over the sound. "She's got herself all worked up about me feeding that cat—and it don't do nobody no harm. Don't you worry none about Mrs. Baylor, *ché*. You just ignore her and let her fuss."

"Um," Madalyn said intelligently. She was surprised. Mom and Daddy didn't like people sometimes—Madalyn could tell Daddy really hadn't liked the principal at Robinson Howard Middle School—but both of her parents made a big deal about Madalyn "being respectful," even when she was mad. They never even let her call Avery's brother, Antony, names, and he was *truly* annoying.

"So, you *do* feed the cat? Mrs. Baylor is right?" Madalyn asked, crossing the room and leaning against the back of the couch.

"I *might*." Papa Lobo drew out the word, giving Madalyn a sidelong glance. "But don't you concern yourself. That's grown folks' business."

Grown folks' business. Sometimes Daddy told Madalyn to stay out of grown folks' conversations at home, so this was probably another way of saying the same thing. Madalyn sighed, watching Papa Lobo continue to scrape at the wall. It was disappointing not to get any more information when she was sure there was a story behind Mrs. Baylor's fussing.

"Oh!" Madalyn said abruptly, as the messy clumps of damp white paper on the tarp behind the couch suddenly made sense. "Papa Lobo! You're taking down the wallpaper?"

"I am," Papa Lobo said, picking up the plastic bottle next to him and spraying the wall again. Madalyn sniffled again at the sweet-sharp smell—was it vinegar? "Your mama said I oughta do something about this front room."

"Ohhhh," Madalyn said slowly, suddenly reminded of the last conversation she'd had with her mother. Her voice wavered. "Um, did she call you? Mom . . . can't come today, so—"

"So, you could put on a T-shirt and come help me rip off this mess," Papa Lobo finished. "She'll be here come Sunday, *ché*. May as well see how much trouble we can get up to before then."

Madalyn hesitated; her nose wrinkled at the smell, but she was intrigued by the soppy, gluey pieces of wallpaper Papa Lobo was slowly pulling away from the wall. Revealed beneath the paper was nasty green paint, the color of rotten avocados. "Um . . . I should do my homework," she began.

The front door banged open. "*Paren*, where y'at?" Jean called. "I brought ice cream."

"Well, c'mon and get yourself some dessert, *ché*," Papa Lobo said, wiping his hands as Jean waved a grocery bag at them through the accordion doors. "You can help me out later on."

It turned out to be pretty hard to ignore the voices from the front room, and all the laughter. Madalyn had decided that Aria was right, and doing her homework first thing Friday afternoon was kind of terrible.

Putting on an old T-shirt and faded pajama shorts, Madalyn had jumped into the unpapering party, standing in a line between Papa Lobo and Jean with her own spray bottle of vinegar and fabric softener, and a paint scraper to pry the thick old paper from the wall. Papa Lobo had brought in a paint-spattered radio and sang oldies in a nice-sounding voice that reminded Madalyn of her daddy and made her smile while also feeling a little bit homesick. Occasionally, a song reminded him of a story, and he told Jean and her things about people and places from long ago—one about Madalyn's father when he was just a kid.

Even Jean was funny and nice—he listened politely when Madalyn talked about school, and he mentioned that last year, Ms. Furukawa's streak had been purple instead of green. He told stories about his father, who was away on a navy ship, much farther away from him than Madalyn's daddy in Massachusetts. Madalyn felt strangely comforted that she wasn't the only one whose family was stretched out all over the place.

The front room, even with the curtains open, was deep in shadows by the time Jean went home for dinner. Between the three of them, they had cleared away almost the entire tree mural, with just a few bits in the high corners left to peel. Jean had talked Papa Lobo into agreeing to take down the wood panels as well, though he'd had to promise he'd be the one to spackle the walls to cover where the nails had been.

Madalyn was getting excited about the whole thing. Papa Lobo had dropped a sheet over the tangle of end tables and assorted roosters, but really, all of them needed wrapping and boxing away, so the painting could begin. The only wall Madalyn had ever gotten to paint was for a wooden backdrop for a play in elementary school—renters weren't always allowed to paint inside rental houses. Madalyn hoped to talk Papa Lobo into something nice like a pale blue, or, if he missed his trees, a forest shade of green.

Papa Lobo had gone into the kitchen to start dinner, and Madalyn was deciding whether she had time for a long shower when she heard a soft scuffing sound and a sharp knock. "Just a sec," Madalyn called, seeing a smallish figure moving down the front walk.

It was hardly the promised "sec" to get through the pushed-together end tables, tangle of lamps, loose roosters, and tchotchkes. She barked her shin on the arm of the couch and gave an annoyed grunt as she flung open the front door.

"Yes, may I help—?"

The woman on the front step had already turned

around and made her way to the driveway, her twig-thin legs moving briskly beneath her long skirt. At first Madalyn thought it was the garden lady from across the street, but this woman's hair was in a silver-gray braid instead of a white one, and her sun hat was smaller. "Hello," the old lady called, her softly rounded face creasing with a smile. "Just left Mr. Thomas some things. You have a nice night, now."

Madalyn scooped up a small gray utility box, jammed with a small pair of garden shears, a knotted length of twine, a folded shirt, and a trowel with a taped handle. Now the woman was well down the street, but she paused a moment to wrestle a weed from a crack in the sidewalk.

Madalyn took advantage of her pause to come all the way down the stairs. "Um, excuse me," she called. "Who should I tell Papa—er, Mr. Thomas—this came from?"

The lady straightened from her weeding and smiled, showing her dimples in her seamed brown skin. "Oh, he'll know, my dear. They're his tools."

"Oh! Okay." Madalyn's answering smile was confused. "Thanks, I guess."

But Madalyn was speaking to the air. The woman with her straight-backed stride had crossed the street and vanished—into Mrs. Baylor's garden!

Madalyn wished she could be a bird and fly over the garden gate. Who *was* the other lady? Was she friends with Mrs. Baylor *and* Papa Lobo? How would that even work?!

Madalyn stood with the door open for so long that Papa Lobo yelled down the hall, "We got money to air-condition the outdoors now? C'mon in here and eat your dinner."

Shaking her head, Madalyn brought in the tools and closed the door.

The next morning, Madalyn woke up late. After a quick shower, she texted a little with Avery, finished her math homework, and then browsed the Highland County Public Library's ebooks to see if they had different books than her county library at home. She was happy to discover that she could still use her own library card to download a book to read. Madalyn sat in the comfortable chair in her bedroom to finish first one, and then another of her favorite series.

At lunch, Madalyn curled herself into the little loveseat in the kitchen nook by the back door. While eating a bowl of cereal, she checked out another library book, one she hadn't read, then finally made herself do the rest of her homework. She didn't want any distractions from Mom on Sunday.

Eventually, Papa Lobo settled into his recliner for a nap, and the quiet pushed Madalyn herself into a light doze, until the recliner's footrest thumped to the floor. "Well. Better get ready to go," Papa Lobo said, pushing himself to his feet.

Madalyn struggled out of the soft couch where she'd sunk into her nap. "Go?" she echoed, blinking. "Where?"

He squinted at her, rasping his hand down his stubbled chin. "Services."

Church? Madalyn rubbed her face, trying to remember the last time she'd gone. Grandpa Collie's wife, Miss Peach, had taken her to confession and Mass last Easter when they visited. Daddy went to services at Christmas, but not usually any other time. Papa Lobo was still looking at Madalyn, his scruffy brow lifted. "Oh," she blurted. "I'm going, too?"

"Sure, you can." Papa Lobo smiled, as if she'd asked to come.

Wait! What? "I—"

"Get a move on, *ché*, don't want to be late," Papa Lobo said, and grinned.

Grumbling a little, Madalyn went into her room.

It was too hot to mess with trying to comb out her hair, so she twisted it into a bun and secured it with a scrunchie. The T-shirt she wore didn't have any words or smudges, and her shorts had a ruffle, so that was kind of fancy. Madalyn tucked her shirt in and shoved her feet into flip-flops. She stepped into the hall before hurrying back to grab a cardigan, just in case. Miss Peach was old-school, and she always made Madalyn wear a cardigan or real sleeves to church, even in Louisiana's muggy heat.

Madalyn brushed her teeth and had a long drink of water before she came back into the front hall, shoving her phone into her back pocket.

"Okay, I'm—"

Madalyn snapped her teeth shut on the word. Last year one of her vocabulary words had been *resplendent*—and that was Papa Lobo just now. His camel-brown suit contrasted with a diamond-print cream-and-white vest, a cream-colored shirt with brown piping on its high collar, and a cream-colored silk tie. His shoes were cream on the top and brown on the sides with pointy toes, and his brown hat was held loosely in his gnarled brown fingers.

"I'm going to go change," Madalyn blurted. Wasn't the five-thirty Vigil Mass casual?

"Don't have time for that," Papa Lobo said mildly, looking over her outfit. "You sure you gonna need that sweater, *mamzél?*"

Madalyn looked down at her flip-flops, then back up at her great-uncle's finery. "I'm . . . I need different shoes. Just a second . . ." Madalyn darted back into her room and emerged at a run, holding up her sparkly flats. Dropping them on the floor, she slid her bare feet into them, then looked up at the old man, who had opened the front door and settled his hat on his shiny head.

"Papa Lobo, aren't you *hot?*"

Papa Lobo held out his arm to her. "Don't matter," he said happily. "I'm *stylin'.*"

Madalyn giggled, observing her great-uncle's straight spine as they matched steps down the front walk. "You are stylin'. You even smell good."

"I do thank you," the old man said, his expression satisfied under the brim of his hat. "A man can enjoy looking fine once a week, can't he, *ché?*"

They walked into the warmth, turning off Gatland Street onto Foothill Road and strolling through the quiet Saturday afternoon in silence, heading toward what looked, at first glance, like an orchard of some kind. And then Madalyn looked up and saw the distinctive domed rooftop of a mission-style church. From this distance, she could see the bell-shaped terraces of two towers and large buildings behind them, including more orchard. They seemed to take up a whole block.

As bells began to ring, Madalyn reluctantly looked at her cardigan, imagining the prickles of perspiration already gathering in her armpits. "Guess we'd better hurry?"

"Nope," Papa Lobo said, and seemed to slow his stroll to a saunter. "Gonna get there right on time," he added, patting her hand.

Wide lawns and rosebushes lined the long driveway into the church grounds. Madalyn noticed that they weren't the only ones walking, but Papa Lobo was the only one so very well dressed—and so very slow. The clock finished chiming its bells, indicating that it was five thirty, and Madalyn winced to see the brown-skinned priest emerge, herding a group of children of various ages who were cinching belts around their green-and-white robes. She and Papa Lobo weren't right on time—they were late.

The priest at the door turned, shading his eyes with his hand. A broad grin split his weathered face, and the breeze ruffled what was left of his thinning, white-streaked hair. "Lorenzo, you're a bit early, aren't you? And who's this young lady?"

"After you, Father Andreas," Papa Lobo said, and winked. "Wouldn't want to upstage anyone. This here is my grand-niece, Madalyn Thomas."

"Well, it's nice to meet you, Madalyn," the priest said, smiling. "You keep that old man in line, all right?"

"Hah! Don't let us keep you, Father." Papa Lobo laughed and gestured toward the door. "Your good flock is waiting. And it's hot as blue blazes out here."

Calm before the Tempest

The church had a cave-like coolness that seeped from the polished granite floors and stone walls, so in the end, Madalyn was glad of her cardigan. There was no choir, but one of the members had brought a guitar and strummed quietly during communion. It was all over in just under an hour. Nothing about it was as stressful as Madalyn remembered—her stepgrandma, Miss Peach, wasn't pinching every time she fidgeted, for one thing—but the minute the last prayer was spoken, Papa Lobo was herding her out of the pew, down the front step, and across the drive.

"Um, that was nice," Madalyn said as they walked

home in the slanting late-afternoon sun. "Are we going again tomorrow?"

Papa Lobo grinned. "Nope. Sunday morning's my poker game."

Madalyn blinked. "You'd better not *ever* let Miss Peach hear that."

"Your *granmé* don't bother me," Papa Lobo said. "Let her come all the way out here, and I take the Eucharist any old time she wants to."

Madalyn grinned. Papa Lobo only said that because he knew it wouldn't happen. Miss Peach liked to travel, but she viewed the entire West Coast as a shaky place about to be rattled into the Pacific Ocean by an earthquake. She would *never* come out to Sheldon just to make her brother-in-law go to church.

"How come you wanted to be late?" Madalyn asked, curiosity roused again. "The priest was actually waiting for you!"

Papa Lobo cleared his throat importantly. "Father Andreas and I have an understanding."

Madalyn giggled. "You mean he understands you're going to be late and leave early?"

"Just never you mind," Papa Lobo said, tilting up his chin to a lofty angle. "*Bondyeu* understands me, and that's all you need to know."

Madalyn repeated the word in her head until it turned into "*bon Dieu*," and shrugged. The Good Lord probably did understand, but she didn't. At least it was something to do, though.

"You know what you oughta do," Papa Lobo said, finally removing his hat and swiping the sheen of sweat off his forehead with his handkerchief. "You oughta go on down to the Fareway and get me some more ice cream."

"Didn't Jean just bring some yesterday? You had root beer floats, remember?"

"He did, at that," Papa Lobo said, cheering up suddenly. His pace increased. "Well, then, let's get some, girl, and get out of this heat."

Sunday morning, Madalyn planned to be standing in the front yard, waiting for her mother when she arrived after lunch, but just after dinner Saturday night she'd ridden her bike to the library and come home, sweaty, with her entire backpack stuffed with new books. She'd taken a shower and put on a big T-shirt and her newest shorts, only to wake up after midnight, fully dressed with a book over her face, extremely grumpy that she'd had to get up just so she could turn off the light and go to bed all over again.

She hadn't gotten nearly enough sleep, and Madalyn had barely pulled herself out of bed by the time
Papa Lobo knocked on her door at nine.

"Ey, *mamzèl*, good morning to you. We ran out of
eggs, and I got folk coming here for breakfast in a bit.
You want to ride out to the Fareway with me?"

"Oh, sure," Madalyn said, shoving her feet into her
flip-flops and pulling down her shirt. "Who's coming
for breakfast?"

Papa Lobo grabbed a pair of canvas bags. "Told ya I
had my poker game, didn't I?"

Poker at breakfast? Sleepily, Madalyn followed
Papa Lobo out the front door, expecting him to take
out his keys and open the door to the truck parked
in the carport. She blinked when Papa Lobo instead
went around to the side of the house and rolled out an
old-fashioned black bike with wide tires and a big basket. Hurriedly, Madalyn went around to the side gate
and brought out her own bike, gathering her messy
hair into a pouf so her bike helmet would fit.

Papa Lobo started out slowly, and the two rode side
by side in silence. The morning was breezy, but a thin
layer of white mist lay between them and the cloud-
less blue sky. Papa Lobo scowled upward. "Just look at
all that smoke," he said.

"That's smoke?" Madalyn blurted, startled out of her sleepy thoughts.

"Can't smell it yet, but it's from those fires up north."

"Oh," Madalyn said, lapsing back into silence. It seemed like there were always fires in California somewhere.

"We'll be lucky if that wind don't drive it down this direction," Papa Lobo continued. "The firefighters got their hands full. Folks need to be more careful."

At the store, the dozen eggs turned into three dozen, plus two cartons of orange-mango juice, a bunch of chives, an eight-ounce carton of chocolate oat milk—for Madalyn, because Papa Lobo saw her looking at it—a couple of baskets of late blackberries, and some whipped topping. By the time they went through the checkout, Madalyn was much more awake, and starving.

Papa Lobo handed Madalyn the milk before carefully placing his canvas bags into the basket on his bike. He munched a few blackberries as they pedaled along.

"So, are we having omelets?" Madalyn asked.

"You makin' omelets?" Papa Lobo asked, giving Madalyn a sly glance.

"I could," Madalyn said, lifting her chin.

Papa Lobo chuckled. "Bet you could, *ché*. Wasn't gonna do no omelets, but I tell you what—you be my short-order cook. Anybody wants one, you fire up your skillet, all right?"

"Okay!" Madalyn said eagerly. She would make hers first, of course, with a tiny bit of cheese and green onions, and then avocado on top, almost like the breakfast burritos Daddy made her at home. She hoped Papa Lobo would save the whipped topping for the blackberries—they looked really good. It would be a great breakfast for her first weekend not at home.

When they got back to the house, Madalyn was surprised to see Jean lugging folding chairs onto the front porch.

"What's he doing?" Madalyn asked.

"Setting up," Papa Lobo said, then hollered at Jean, "Ey, *fiyo*. Brought you some doughnuts, in the house."

Madalyn's mouth watered. Doughnuts? When had Papa Lobo gone to the bakery?

"All right!" Jean said happily.

"Coulda had you some chocolate milk, but this one drank it right out the carton like she don't have no home training," Papa Lobo continued, pointing his thumb at Madalyn, then let out a huge laugh as Madalyn sputtered.

"What? I—you—"

Chortling, he opened the side gate and wheeled his bike into the side yard.

Madalyn found herself shy as a vigorous knock sounded at the front door a few minutes later. She retreated into the kitchen and fiddled with the apron Papa Lobo had given her. They had set the scarred wooden table for six, and a big pink bakery box had pride of place in the middle of the table. Madalyn fiddled with the napkins and straightened the edges of the forks, stalling. She didn't want to go outside.

On the porch, she could hear voices and laughter, and she crossed her arms over the weird feeling in her stomach. Jean knew all Papa Lobo's friends and was outside in the middle of everything. Sundays at Madalyn's house were quiet—with the newspaper and coffee and family—they were nothing like this.

"Madalyn!" She heard Papa Lobo's bellow a few minutes later. "C'mon out here, *ché*."

Swallowing, Madalyn went to the front of the house and stepped onto the porch. Three old men sat at a sturdy card table, grinning mischievous grins. Stacks of cards and colorful poker chips sat at one end, and a forest of glass bottles sat on the other. A coffee urn crouched on a rickety piano bench near the house, its short cord dangling.

Papa Lobo was bending over one of the bottles with Jean, but he waved Madalyn over. "Come on out and meet the boys."

Boys? Madalyn took in a dark-skinned, balding man with sleepy eyes and two-toned suede loafers; a white-haired, heavyset gentleman with age spots freckling the large, pale hands clasped over his cane; and a thin, brown-skinned gentleman in a striped sports coat and a fedora, who flashed a gold crown in his smile. These were the oldest boys Madalyn had ever seen! But Papa Lobo smiled proudly and set a heavy hand on Mada-lyn's shoulder as he turned her toward them. "This here's Madalyn, my *neveu*—my nephew—Paul's girl. She stays with me now. Madalyn, you remember Doc, and this is Mario and Warren."

Madalyn shook hands with the man with the cane—Doc. She did remember Dr. Buchannan—he was Papa Lobo's friend who'd stopped by to look at the scrape on her leg on the first day of school. He had given her a flexible brown bandage and a lollipop—as if she were six. Madalyn smiled self-consciously and waved to the other men, not sure who was who, but the one she thought was Mario took off his hat and bowed over her hand, making Madalyn feel giggly and embarrassed. Papa Lobo didn't even stick around to make sure Madalyn said "nice to meet you" to everyone or anything. He was much more casual about introductions than Mom and Daddy were.

"Give it another drop of blue." Papa Lobo had turned back now to Jean and the bottles of . . . something. Madalyn stepped closer. Daddy and Mom didn't drink alcohol, but Madalyn had seen bottles like these before at Avery's house on special occasions. But what were they doing?

Jean put down a tiny bottle of food coloring, stuck his thumb over the mouth of the bottle, and gave it a quick shake.

"Better?"

"Looks just like that blue gin," the bald man with the cute shoes said with a satisfied nod.

"Sapphire," Doc corrected him.

"Looks blue to me," the man with the hat argued.

Jean caught Madalyn's confused glance and grinned.

Madalyn felt a little worried. So, gin was another alcohol, right? Were you supposed to add color to it? What her mother had said about Papa Lobo's poker friends echoed through her mind. Were they going to start swearing and smoking cigars next? Why was Jean laughing? "Um . . . Can someone explain—?"

Madalyn began, but Papa Lobo hushed her, patting the air between them.

"Shh, now! Here they come."

Madalyn leaned against the porch railing as Papa Lobo shoved glass tumblers into the hands of his friends. The man with the cane poured the blue liquid into his glass and raised it to Madalyn with a wink.

The man with the gold tooth—Mario—cleared his throat and said loudly, "Now, did I ever tell you all about the time I went fishing in San Juan and caught a fifty-foot marlin?"

"I don't remember you telling that lie," Doc said, opening a deck of cards and giving them a fancy shuffle.

"Lie? I never lie!" Mario sounded offended, but his eyes were smiling as he resettled his hat and leaned back in his seat. "Well, listen. See, what happened was—"

"Well, I *never*!" The deep voice smacked into Madalyn's ears like a slap, and she jumped, startled into tripping over her feet. Madalyn edged around the table toward Papa Lobo as Mrs. Baylor sailed toward the mailbox wearing a huge scowl and an even bigger hat. The flowers on its brim quivered with her emphatic words. "No one *civilized* would be *drinking* and *gambling* at this hour in the morning. Young Mr. Duval, you should be more careful of the company you keep." Mrs. Baylor sniffed, as if she'd smelled something terrible, then turned to Madalyn, lifting her chin like an elegant swan ignoring a pond full of ducks. "Good morning, Madalyn. May I invite you to attend services with me this morning?"

Madalyn's eyes widened. "Oh! Good morning, Mrs. Baylor. Um." She glanced at Papa Lobo, who patted her on the arm. "Thank you, but we went to Mass last night. Right now, we're going to have brunch. Um . . . maybe another time."

"Yes, of course, dear," Mrs. Baylor said, as if she'd expected Madalyn's answer. "You have a lovely day, now."

A pair of women bustled up the sidewalk behind Mrs. Baylor. One stepped forward to touch her arm, smiling up at the gathering on the porch. She wore her hair tucked under a hat, but Madalyn recognized her. She was the woman who had come to return Papa Lobo's tools. "Good morning, all. We don't want to be late, Sister," she said, and tugged Mrs. Baylor's arm.

"Of course not. And I think it's high time I spoke with Father Andreas about the examples being set in our community," Mrs. Baylor added, giving the men on the porch a sharp look. She stalked off down the street, walking so fast that the other ladies had to trot a little to keep up with her.

Madalyn stared after them, then turned to look at Papa Lobo.

"We're bad examples?"

Madalyn's question seemed overly loud in the silence on the front porch, and she slapped a hand over her mouth. "I mean," she began, but the silence broke with wheezing laughter, which started small and then rose to a chorus of hearty guffaws.

"That's just Mrs. Baylor, fussing about me." Papa Lobo patted Madalyn's arm again. "Don't let her bother you."

"She nearly busted a vein this time," Mario wheezed.

"Just once, we need to get Father Andreas out here with us," the man with the nice shoes said, and chuckled evilly.

"Naw, Warren, that'd give her a stroke," Doc said comfortably, pushing up with his cane. "And I can't support that, seeing as I still have the Hippocratic oath to uphold. Lo, I'm ready to eat."

"Doc, you always ready to eat," Papa Lobo answered, to more laughter. He stood and scooped up the cards. The other men pitched in to clear the table of chips, then followed him inside, insulting each other and laughing.

Madalyn lingered on the porch watching Jean, who was collecting the bottles and dumping the colorful liquid out on the worn boards. Startled, Madalyn grabbed the nearest bottle and sniffed at the liquid.

Jean glanced at her. "It's just water."

"Water?"

Jean rubbed his chin and straightened. "Yep."

Madalyn waited, but Jean didn't explain. "Well? Does Papa Lobo do this every Sunday? Is Mrs. Baylor always mad? Why didn't they play poker? What's going on, Jean?"

Jean shrugged. "It's just *Paren* messing with Mrs. Baylor. They've been fussing at each other a long time."

"But why, though?" Madalyn held up the bottle of pink-colored liquid. It was so pretty she hated to dump it out. "Why does Papa Lobo get her all mad on purpose?"

Jean looked sheepish. "Well . . . I started it."

"*You?*" Madalyn's eyes were wide.

Jean shrugged. "It was dumb. . . . A bunch of us were kicking rocks in the parking lot after services when we were, like, ten. Mrs. Baylor saw us fooling around, and she told Father Andreas that I kicked a rock and scratched her car."

Madalyn gaped. "Jean!"

"I didn't!" Jean dumped another bottle over the edge of the porch rail and glanced back at Madalyn. "I swear, it wasn't me. I know who did, but it wasn't me. And I told Mom and Father Andreas it wasn't me, and Papa Lobo told Mrs. Baylor it wasn't me, but she wouldn't believe it. She threw a big old fit, so Mom paid for her to get that little tiny scratch fixed. I got in so much trouble! I had to wash cars all summer to pay Mom back."

"Oh," Madalyn said, making a face. "That's not fair."

"Eh. I shouldn't have been kicking rocks anyway," Jean said, and shrugged. "Thing is, even after everything got fixed, Mrs. Baylor still got on my case about *everything*. Every time something went wrong in the whole neighborhood, if a window got broken or someone lit firecrackers or wrote graffiti on something, Mrs. Baylor would look down her nose and say it was probably me, and that got *Paren* upset. They argued all the time."

"Oh," Madalyn said unhappily. She couldn't imagine nice Mrs. Baylor acting that way. "But . . . she's really nice to *me*. She always waves at me from her garden if she's outside."

"Yeah, she's all right if she likes you," Jean said, gathering another pair of bottles. "But if she doesn't— watch out. When *Paren* put up a squirrel feeder, she got on his case for 'feeding rodents.' He started feeding that cat instead—and that got Mrs. Baylor fussing even worse. She complained about *Paren*'s lawn, and when he took it out and put in rocks, she complained about that." Jean shook his head. "The only thing she cares about is that garden of hers, and just because *Paren*'s got better things to do than mess around with flowers like she does, she can't stand him. They're never going to be friends." Jean collected the last of his bottles and opened the front door. "My advice? If you ever see them fussing at each other, just get out of the way."

Cloudy with a Hint of Silver

"Check," **Mr. Duchamps** said, leaning back and rearranging the cards in his hand.

The quiet shuffle of cards punctuated the stillness of the afternoon as the other players reconsidered the hands in front of them. A clink of melting ice from Doc's iced coffee was the loudest sound as the glass sweated in the warm room.

The deep white sink was piled with plates where the eggs, bacon, and potato fritters the bald Mr. Duchamps had brought had disappeared as if someone had called a race and said, "Go!" Madalyn snuck a sip of Papa Lobo's coffee and nibbled another bite of apple fritter to chase the bitterness of the hot black liquid away.

She was never going to finish the huge doughnut, but it had looked too delicious to leave alone.

"I call," Mr. Mendoza said with a loud sigh, and put a stack of pennies on the table.

Madalyn leaned over and looked at Papa Lobo's cards. He angled them toward her, raising his eyebrows. Madalyn nodded seriously, and Papa Lobo nodded back. "I raise," he stated, and added another stack of pennies to the table.

Across the table, Jean snorted.

"What?" Madalyn glared at Jean. Papa Lobo was teaching her to play poker, but Jean acted like she was too dumb to learn. "What's so funny?" she asked.

Jean rolled his eyes and shook his head. "Nothing."

Madalyn carefully reorganized Papa Lobo's pennies into neat stacks. She didn't really know exactly what she was doing, but she'd listened carefully as Papa Lobo had told her which cards were important and which weren't. She wasn't sure exactly about all the rules, and she didn't know why Doc sometimes laughed under his breath before he put down his cards, but she was learning. So far, they hadn't lost, anyway.

"Don't you worry about Jean, *ché*," Papa Lobo murmured. "He—"

"Hello in there. Anybody home?" Madalyn startled.

The knocking on the door was loud.

"C'mon through," Papa Lobo hollered, and smiled over at Madalyn. "Well, *mamzèl*, your mama finally managed to make her way on over here."

Madalyn could barely untangle herself from the chair before Mom came into the kitchen with a bag of groceries and a big smile, which brightened as she saw Madalyn at the table full of poker chips and cards.

"Mom!"

"Hey, babe! Hey, Uncle Lo, hello, everyone, sorry for interrupting," Mom apologized, swooping in and hugging Madalyn, and waving Papa Lobo and the other men down as they stood politely to greet her. "Hello again, Jean. Everyone, I'm Macie Thomas, Madalyn's mother. Lo, I brought some extra groceries for next week, I'll just—"

Mom broke off as she glanced around for a place to set down her bag. Her eyes moved over to the sink, where Jean had rinsed out the liquor bottles and turned them upside down into the drainer.

Madalyn followed her mother's gaze, noting the presence of the little wrinkle between her eyebrows. "They put colored water in the bottles, Mom," she said quickly. "It was for a joke."

"Uh-*huh*," Mom said, one eyebrow arching high on

her forehead. "I'm sure I don't even want to know, do I?" she muttered, as the men around the table laughed. Smiling, she unloaded avocados, bags of fruit, more of Madalyn's lactose-free cheese, oat milk, and a dozen eggs onto the counter. "Let me just put these away, and you can come out and shoot the breeze with me about your week."

Papa Lobo offered Mom his "special vegetarian" bacon—which was just regular bacon—toast, and coffee. Madalyn offered to make her mother an omelet. Mom waved away all the fuss and made herself a cup of unsweetened tea, then added ice. She also stole Madalyn's doughnut. The two of them went out onto the back porch to sit in the shade and catch up by Papa Lobo's gardenia bushes.

"It was a good week, mostly," Madalyn was saying, settling back into the plastic deck chair with her water bottle. "The vampires—Carlin and Sydney—have kind of turned out to be okay. I'm not sure what to do about Natalie, but . . . she hasn't said anything else, and she's still really nice, so I guess . . . I don't know."

"It sounded like a really confusing thing to have happen," her mother agreed in her Social Worker Voice. "I think you're doing the best thing you can do for Natalie. Just listen to her when she wants to talk.

She has to work out how she feels her own way. You don't have to agree with what she says, but it sounds like the best way you can be a friend is to listen."

"I guess." Madalyn sighed. She had already texted her mom most of the story, and it was weird to talk about now, instead of a little at a time every day. "It's okay, Mom. I don't think—ooh, hey, kitty!"

The small gray cat that had so annoyed Mrs. Baylor was mincing along the top of the back fence. She jumped down onto Papa Lobo's rocking chair and meowed at them loudly.

"I think she wants food," Madalyn said, and looked at her doughnut.

"No, don't feed animals people food," Mom reminded her. "I'm sure we shouldn't feed her at all. Someone is probably missing her at home. She has a collar, see?"

"Oh." Madalyn leaned forward and peeked at the white collar around the cat's neck. The cat's fur was so bushy that Madalyn could barely see it. "I'm glad she has a collar. I don't know whose cat she is, but somebody should tell her owner that the lady across the street *really* doesn't like her." And then Madalyn had to tell her mother all about Mrs. Baylor, her amazing garden, and then how she was so chilly toward Jean and Papa Lobo that morning. Mom was giving the cat skritches under the chin by the time Madalyn got to where they'd added the food coloring to the bottles.

"Papa Lobo isn't what Mrs. Baylor thinks," Madalyn said. "He was just pretending. He went to church, and Father Andreas didn't even care that he was almost late. But . . . Mrs. Baylor isn't what Papa Lobo thinks she is, either," Madalyn explained. "They're both so nice, but . . . just not to each other."

"I can see that," Mom said, and shook her head. "He and his friends are having a good laugh, but it sounds like what they really need to is sit down and have a good talk to clear the air. Not everyone in the neighborhood has to be best friends, but I'd hate to see something more serious come out of this picking on each other."

"I know," Madalyn said. "I didn't think Papa Lobo would do something to make someone mad on purpose . . . I didn't think adults had big fights like that."

Mom muttered something under her breath about maturity, then sighed. "*Most* adults probably don't. Uncle Lorenzo is just . . . one of a kind."

"That's probably a good thing." Madalyn giggled, then straightened. "Oh! Guess what? We're taking down the wallpaper in the front room and redoing it!"

"You are?" Mom sat up, and her eyes got wide.

"That's *great*. Let's see it!"

"Don't get too excited—we just got started," Mada-lyn said, leaping up and startling the cat into skittering under the chair. "Papa Lobo and Jean used vinegar and fabric softener to soften up the glue, and I scraped it off. It smells really weird, and it's worse when it's hot. I was going to work on it this afternoon, but . . ."

"Maybe we can start again when it cools down," Mom said, grabbing her glass off the table and fol-lowing Madalyn to the door. "I don't care how it smells—anything's better than smoke. That's what it smells like at home. There's a big fire in Somerset, and there's been a lot of awful smoke smell in the air all week long. I'm so glad it's clear here."

"Avery said there's fires near Winters, too," Madalyn said in a low voice as they went through the kitchen full of people and out into the hall. "It's bothering her brother's asthma."

"All those gorgeous trees up there," Mom said sadly. "I can't understand why people are so careless."

Madalyn folded back the front room doors and ges-tured dramatically. "Ta-da!"

Her mother recoiled and coughed a little. "Oof— you were right, it does smell odd. At least you left the windows open." She moved a little way into the room then turned, eyes scanning the walls and the chaotic jumble of disordered furniture and roosters. "I can imagine this with the walls a really pale yellow and the rest of that awful wood paneling off the wall. . . . You know, babe, I'm glad you're helping out Uncle Lo. It's good to see you keeping busy, and I'm sure the old man appreciates it."

A loud roar of laughter came just then from the rear of the house, and Mom jumped, turning to glance guiltily over her shoulder. Madalyn giggled. "Old man. I dare you to say that loud enough for him to hear."

"Well, he *is* old," Mom said, and smiled, but it wasn't a real smile that filled up her whole face. She had that same little wrinkle in between her eyebrows.

"Is something wrong?" Madalyn blurted.

"Now, what would make you say that?" Mom asked, the little wrinkle getting deeper.

"You . . . look funny." Madalyn swallowed and added, "Maybe worried or something?"

Her mother laughed a little. "You've got sharp eyes, kiddo." She smiled. "Just a few clouds on the horizon."

Madalyn ignored the cloud talk. "Is it Daddy?"

"No—your father is fine, just great." Mom rolled her lips in against her teeth, looking like she was thinking hard. "Madalyn," she said slowly, "you've had a pretty good weekend here, haven't you?"

Madalyn frowned, answering slowly, "It was . . . okay."

"This looks like you've been keeping busy," Mom said, gesturing to the walls and the room. "You said Uncle Lo sang with you, and told jokes?"

"Yeah," Madalyn said, crossing her arms. She didn't have a good feeling about this.

Mom leaned against the doorframe and took a breath. "Well, I'm thinking about picking up some extra hours at work," she began, and Madalyn stiffened.

"When?"

"Just on the weekends your dad doesn't come home. Some of our ombudsmen have started putting in a few hours here and there, and they could use some extra on-call staff to man the phones sometimes."

Madalyn's face crumpled. "*What?* But Mom—"

"It's just something to think about," Mom said, reaching out to smooth a hand over Madalyn's hair. She pulled her closer into an awkward hug, her arm going around Madalyn's neck and choking her a little bit. "Just hear me out, okay? I know you want to be back in your own room, and I know staying here would mean you and I don't get to see each other as much every weekend. But it would be temporary—our office expanded into Solano County, and so we have quite a few new hires, and there's just a lot to be done. It would be much nicer for you to be here, with Papa Lobo, with the library right there, and a bit of company, than in an empty house by yourself, right?"

Madalyn grunted, trying to cuddle close but needing to breathe. "Do you *have* to?"

"It's a good idea, babe," Mom said, her voice muffled as she pressed her cheek against the top of Madalyn's head. "The time your dad was out of work put a big dent in our savings, and even though things are a lot better now, the more we can put away for next time, the better. Think about where you want to stay—here or there—and we'll talk about it again tonight, okay?"

"Fine," Madalyn said glumly. Daddy had been looking for work for almost seven months, and Madalyn knew her parents had been worrying about money for just that long. She slumped and tried not to grind her teeth. Madalyn knew what she had to say. She knew it, but she didn't like it. She would have to stay.

Her mother squeezed Madalyn more tightly, then held her away from her embrace so that she could look right into Madalyn's eyes. "Just think about it, Madalyn, all right? It won't be forever. I promise." She squeezed her daughter again. "And if you stay here, at least you'll get to help throw out the roosters, right?"

"I guess," Madalyn said, but she wasn't ready to join her mother in smiling. She wasn't going to be a baby about this, but Madalyn wasn't sure she'd be able to smile about it for a long, long time.

High-Pressure System

"**How's my baby** girl?" Daddy asked.

Madalyn looked away from the little circle of her phone's camera and shrugged. "Okay."

"Ooh," her father said. "It's like that, huh?"

"What?" Madalyn asked, scowling. "I didn't say anything."

"Sometimes not saying anything is saying something," Daddy said, eyebrows raised.

"Whatever." Madalyn rolled her eyes. Daddy trying to be deep was *so* annoying. "I said I was okay."

Her mother had left Madalyn to talk to Daddy on the phone while she and Papa Lobo "caught up." Madalyn knew that meant they were talking about her, probably. Even though she pretty much knew every-thing they were going to say (probably?) and knew all the reasons Mom had decided to work more, there was a part of her that was still feeling sulky and mad. She wished she weren't too old to sit under a table and pout, like she'd done when she was five. This wasn't *fair*. Hadn't she put up with enough? First Robinson Howard. Now this.

"Babe. Talk to me, now. Mom said you were having a hard time," Daddy said seriously.

Madalyn shrugged again and sighed. "I'm all right, Daddy."

Her father smiled and leaned too close to the cam-era, so all Madalyn could see was his nose hairs, and not the weird green walls in the studio apartment he was renting in Cambridge. "You thought about what you want to do next weekend?"

Madalyn shrugged again, and then, wondering if her father could actually see her, she decided to use her words. "Nope."

"But we'll all be together—don't you have stuff you want to do? We'll go out to breakfast at The Mad Platter, and maybe get down to the bookstore," Daddy suggested.

"Unless you're too tired," Madalyn said, and Daddy

laughed a little, rubbing his hand over his chest as if it hurt there.

"Ah, babe, don't be too hard on your old dad. Listen—I'm gonna make sure I'm not too tired, all right?" he insisted. "I'll sleep on the plane or something. Look, I know with us spending so much time apart, things aren't the way we want them. But we'll just have to make the time we have count, okay?"

"Yeah, okay," Madalyn said, but even she could hear she didn't sound very convincing. So she tried. She'd told Daddy everything she'd told Mom—all over again. She told him about how funny Aria was, and about Wendy's gorgeous hair. She told him about Natalie's nails, and he told her he didn't think it would break the bank if she got herself a couple of bottles of polish and some stickers like Natalie's. Madalyn just shrugged. She wasn't sure she wanted nail polish, not really.

She told Daddy about Jean, and the colored water, and all the things that Mrs. Baylor had said. Her description of what the old men had said after made her father laugh, which was the best thing, but by the time Madalyn got off the phone, she was so tired, she just lay down on the bed.

Trying to make other people feel good when she felt so bad took a lot of energy.

Riding her bike to school with Mom the next morning—Mom had borrowed Papa Lobo's heavy, black bike with the big tires—even though it was cool with a thin layer of clouds, Madalyn waved at Mrs. Baylor in her garden, feeling slow and grumpy. She was sleepy, the light looked weird, it was too windy, and Mom's chitchat was on her *last* nerve.

"Just look at the sky . . . do you see how everything is kind of yellowy? That's from smoke—there's a fire somewhere down here, too," Mom said, and coughed. Her bike wobbled. "This so-called fire season is the worst. Since when is it a 'season' when it's not brought on by nature? But here we are again with fires, every single year," she grumbled.

Madalyn rolled her eyes. Mom said something like that every single year, every time a grass fire threatened green spaces, woods, and national parks. "When are people going to see our climate is changing? It's not just a few leaves, or folks not putting out their campfires," her mother continued, raising her eyebrows emphatically at Madalyn.

"Yep," Madalyn said, and pedaled a little ahead.

"All right, I see I'd better change the subject, since it's hard to stand on my soapbox while I'm riding this heavy old bike," Mom said, and laughed. She caught up to Madalyn and reached across the space between them to touch her arm. "I'm glad to see you're doing so well with your math," she said, steering closer. "That's a real silver lining to having to change schools—you've got a great teacher. I left a message for Mrs. Solazzo letting her know we appreciate her."

"Yep," Madalyn said, watching her mother's front wheel wobble as she coughed again. She wasn't very good at doing two things at once. Mom had said she hadn't ridden a bike for about thirteen years, but *still*.

"Try to think if there's anything you need from home next weekend. It's still so hot—" Mom looked up at the blue-and-white sky. "I was going to suggest we get out some cold-weather clothes, but even though it's windy, I think you might still be in shorts for a while."

"Uh-huh." More and more kids filled the sidewalks and the road around them. Mom was still talking— she pedaled *so* slow!—and now Madalyn could see the school. "Mom," she blurted, interrupting her mother's stream of conversation.

". . . help finish up the front room. I told Uncle Lo that— What?" Mom seemed startled. She steered to the side of the road and squeezed the brakes too hard.

Madalyn slowed and circled back. "I was just going to say, you don't have to go all the way to school with me."

Mom, who had slid off the seat when she braked, climbed back up and balanced her foot against the sidewalk. "What? Madalyn, we're almost there."

"I know . . ." Prickly with embarrassment, Madalyn steered closer. "You can come if you want," she said, feeling a little mean. "I just—I don't *need* you to come. You should just go. To work, I mean. You always complain about traffic."

Mom sighed, then slumped, resting her arms on the handlebars. "There's always traffic," she said, and she looked at Madalyn for a long, silent moment. "I guess you're right. This is just a long goodbye, and we'll have much more time next weekend."

"Yep," Madalyn said, pedaling in another circle.

"We'll plan something fun with your dad—"

"Yep," Madalyn said, pedaling faster.

"And I'll call you tonight. I know this is hard on you, Madalyn. Do you want to come and give me a hug?"

Madalyn coughed, now feeling a catch in her own throat that maybe wasn't from the smoke. "I'm gonna be late, Mom."

Mom half smiled. "Well, I need a hug, even if you don't want to give me one."

Oh. Now Madalyn's wheel was the one to wobble. Her heart felt achy at her mother's words, but she was too out of sorts to kiss and make up, even with Mom. "Uh—"

Her mother smiled and shook her head. "I can see which way the wind's blowing, babe. That's fine. I'll go back and hug Uncle Lorenzo. Be good. I'll see you Friday."

"Wait. Mom—" Madalyn began, wincing with embarrassment as her mother picked up the bike and lugged it around until it was pointing the other direction. Couldn't she even sit on the bike and turn? Balancing on the sidewalk, Mom got back onto the seat, wobbling a little, then pedaled hard, her front wheel straight.

"Have a good day!" her mother called over her shoulder.

"Bye, Mom," Madalyn said, but the smoke—it must have been the smoke—made her throat hurt.

That wasn't the way Madalyn had wanted that conversation with her mother to go.

Unhappily, Madalyn rode the rest of the way to school, a little ball of discomfort growing beneath her ribs. She carried it with her all morning long. Natalie's bright-fuchsia nail polish was too bright. Aria's voice was too loud, and morning announcements over the PA were irritating. Wendy's shoes—new black boots with tiny lavender flowers—were so cute Madalyn wished she'd never seen them, which only made her feel selfish and awful.

Today, Madalyn didn't think Ms. Castaic's fun activity at the beginning of History was very fun. She didn't want to think of three clues about her favorite country, and she didn't want to guess anyone else's favorite country, either. It was annoying when Ms. Furukawa assigned them to create an advertisement or an award for one of the characters in *Julie of the Wolves*. Madalyn had liked the book last week—then it had seemed adventurous and inspiring, but now it seemed like just a lot of snow. Why couldn't she just write a book report like she'd done eight times last year at Robinson Howard Middle School?

Even Mrs. Solazzo's weird outfit—a black skirt with white polka dots worn with striped black-and-white tights, black ballet flats, and a math joke in black writing on a white T-shirt—didn't cheer her up. She was *sick* of word problems. Madalyn didn't care how many yards of ribbon it took to wrap four boxes, or twenty—her birthday was two months away, and anyway, what if Papa Lobo didn't know, and Mom and Daddy forgot, and she didn't *get* presents this year?

She hadn't been very nice this morning, and she probably didn't deserve them.

It was only Math block, but already Madalyn was ready to go back to Papa Lobo's and go back to bed.

Fourth-period lunch at Kingsbridge Junior High was first lunch, which Madalyn usually thought was good. First lunch meant the lunchroom hadn't been used yet, and didn't smell weird, like other people's food. Today it smelled . . . like something burnt. Madalyn screwed up her face as she opened her lunch bag. Cucumber slices and a carrot, peeled and cut into short spears, an egg salad sandwich with sprinkles of bacon bits, and four doughnut holes, leftover from Sunday brunch. Madalyn felt a little surge of happiness, followed by a sour feeling in her stomach. Mom had made her a *good* lunch. Madalyn hadn't even said thank you.

"Gross! What's that smell?" Natalie asked as she came from the lunch line. She had the Monday menu of cheese nachos with beef crumbles and a carton of 2 percent milk. Thick cheese dripped as Natalie picked up a tortilla chip.

Madalyn glared at her. "Well, it's not *my* food," she said.

"I didn't mean *you*," Natalie blurted, eyes widening. "I—I meant . . . I mean, it stinks. In the air."

"It's the fire," Aria said, biting into her apple.

"What fire?" Natalie asked worriedly.

"My mom said the fire's in Somerset," Madalyn disagreed, pulling out her napkin, and frowning when a folded piece of blue paper dropped to the table. "We can't smell fire from all the way over there."

"There is a fire in Somerset," Wendy agreed, plopping her tray down next to Aria. "There's also one in Woodland, and one in Sutter, too," she added, crunching loudly. "That's why we can smell it. It's the wind. All the fires are spreading."

"Oh no. That's really close," said Natalie, her eyes darting as she looked toward the lunchroom doors. They were closed today, because the wind was high. Outside, Madalyn could see the trees shaking their branches.

"It's not even that close," Madalyn said, her voice louder than it needed to be. "Natalie, you worry about everything."

Natalie ducked her head and shoved a chip into her mouth. She didn't say anything.

Aria did, though. "What's up with *you* today?" she asked Madalyn, frowning.

"Nothing," Madalyn muttered. She crumpled the note from Mom and hid it underneath her sandwich. She couldn't bear to open it up and see the words Mom had meant to make her feel good and loved and special when she wasn't feeling like any of those things.

"Are you sure?" Aria asked, squinting a little as she tried looking Madalyn in the eye.

Madalyn ducked her head even lower. She didn't want to be seen right now. "Yeah," she said quickly. "Um . . . I didn't mean it like that, Natalie. Sorry. I just meant . . . if the fire gets bad, they'll tell us. Or cancel school. Or something."

"They'd better," Aria said, then turned suddenly and called out to another table. "Hey—Ian! Are you already doing your homework? That's cheating!"

Slowly, Madalyn ate her lunch. Wendy and Natalie talked to each other and to the other kids around them. Aria got up and walked around the room like she always did, but Madalyn sat, quiet and still. When she had finished her food, she uncrumpled the note from her lunch bag, smoothing out the wrinkles in the paper as she unfolded it.

Hey, Girlie,
If things turn out best for the people who make

the best of things, then you are helping make
things turn out great. I know this separation has
been hard—on your dad and me, too. Thank you for
making it easier.

♥ *Mom*

Madalyn folded the note so fast it crumpled. It felt like she'd swallowed a rock. Papa Lobo was great, and she didn't want to make things harder for Mom and Daddy, but she also really, really, really, *really* hated both of them being away. How could she make the best of that?

Over the loudspeaker, bells played. Madalyn frowned and looked at the big black clock on the wall. "It's not time for next period already!" she protested.

"No, it's way early," Natalie said, twisting to look as well. "This isn't the right music, anyway."

Madalyn nodded. In the morning, the music that played right before morning announcements was from the cartoon *Fantasia*, the part with the dancing broomsticks. This music sounded like a warning, like alarm bells from someone's phone.

"This is a shelter in place," said a voice over the loudspeaker. "Staff and students, move to your shelter areas."

A taste like metal ran across the inside of Madalyn's mouth, and she froze.

Natalie gasped. Across the room, a teacher jumped up, grabbing her tray. Wendy's brown eyes, as she twisted in her seat to stare at Madalyn, were huge. That's why the music had sounded familiar . . . they'd had safety drills the first week of school. These were the bells that came with the emergency announcement. Madalyn gripped the table, waiting for—something. For more words to explain that this was just a drill, like last week.

But the voice just repeated the same sentence, in the same loud voice. "This is a shelter in place. Staff and students, move to your shelter areas."

"Go! Go! Go! Do not run! Walk! Get to the gym!" Now the teacher was yelling, standing, and waving her hands. The double doors to the hallway were open, and other cafeteria staff were standing there, gesturing students to go through. Madalyn curled her toes in her shoes. Her legs felt shaky.

"Come *on*!" Aria said, hurrying by to grab Wendy by the arm. "Don't just sit there! We have to go!"

Madalyn gulped. This felt just like Robinson Howard Middle School all over again, and this time, Mom and Daddy were far, far away.

Red Skies at Morning

No one went back to class after lunch. Everyone had to sit down on the floor in the gym—or wherever they were—and wait.

At first, it had been noisy, as more and more people came in, and everyone whispered and wondered what was happening. Ms. Furukawa had called students' names, but she hadn't had everyone on her list. Then, the vice principal, Mr. Reedy, had come in, and everyone had gotten quiet. He called people's names from his clipboard, and he had everyone. The first time he'd said her name, though, Madalyn hadn't answered loudly enough.

"Madalyn Thomas, are you here?" Mr. Reedy

bellowed, looking out across the room.

"Here!" Madalyn yelled, and then felt her face get hot as Carlin giggled.

"Students, please pay attention," Mr. Reedy had said, narrowing his blue eyes right at Madalyn, and she'd scowled. It wasn't her fault he couldn't hear.

More teachers had come into the gym, and a few of the teachers who didn't have students brought in their laptops and sat on the floor and worked. The cafeteria staff had come around with water bottles and wrapped sandwiches for those who hadn't had lunch, and small bags of animal crackers for everyone else. Mr. Reedy came back and gave a sharp, loud whistle to get people's attention and explained what was going on.

It turned out that the wind had knocked down electrical wires all over the place, and some sparks had set a fire on the other side of town. Because it was hot outside, and windy, the dryness just made the fire worse. It had burned the grass and bushes all over the property, and then a spark had jumped into the grass across the road. Now the air was thick with clouds of smoke and it was hard to see what was only ten feet away. The school was concerned about kids walking home and getting caught in the middle of smoke and ash and fire trucks, so they had to wait until the all clear to go home.

"That's not that bad," Aria said, sitting back with a relieved sigh, but Natalie still looked worried. Natalie looked worried a lot, Madalyn realized.

"What if we can't go home tonight?" Natalie asked.

"Why would they keep us at school?" Wendy wondered, frowning. "It's just a grass fire."

"Well, I don't know. I mean, what if they want an adult to pick us up? Annica can't pick me up; she had meetings in Sacramento all day."

"That's okay, you can come over to my house!" Aria exclaimed.

"I don't know," Wendy said doubtfully. "When it's an emergency, they sometimes only let you go with your parents or guardian or something."

At Natalie's downcast look, Aria offered, "We can stay here with you."

Natalie shook her head. "Thanks, but I'll be okay," she said, her voice glum.

"Wait—I know! Madalyn can stay," Aria interrupted. "She lives the closest."

Madalyn jumped, losing her grip on the paper label she was peeling from her water bottle and turned a wide-eyed look on Aria. Times like these, she *really*

148

missed Avery. Avery would *never* volunteer Madalyn for anything. Why did Aria have to be so . . . helpful?

She was right, Madalyn *did* live closest, but all Madalyn wanted to do was go home and wait for Mom to get off work so they could talk about . . . everything.

But Natalie had no one to hang out with and seemed a little worried. After this week, Madalyn knew how *that* felt, and it wasn't Natalie's fault that Madalyn had been in a strange, snippy mood, was it?

Madalyn held back a sigh. "Um . . . yeah. I can stay with you, Natalie. I have to call first, but I don't think Papa Lobo would mind if I stayed—or if you came over. Papa Lobo's my grandpa's brother," she added at Natalie's curious look.

"So, you live with your great-uncle? Do you not have parents anymore?" Natalie asked.

Wendy widened her eyes. "Natalie!"

"What?" Natalie said, scowling. "I was just asking. Carlin lives with her grandma, not her grandma's sister."

"I have *parents*, Natalie," Madalyn said, rolling her eyes. "I'm staying with Papa Lobo because my dad works on the East Coast, and my mom works a lot of hours in Gold Hill, and they wanted to make sure I had someone at home. Papa Lobo is just helping out."

Aria nudged Madalyn with her shoulder. "That's why my cousin Jaime lives with us. Now he doesn't have to drive so far to get to his job. It's good to help out family."

Madalyn felt a little better—Aria was too friendly sometimes, but at least she understood.

"Well, I live with my sister, not my parents," Natalie said. "And thanks, Madalyn, but I can't go over to anybody's house unless Annica knows them, and I don't talk to boys."

"What boys?" Wendy asked, but they were interrupted by the sound of the alarm bell, and the vice principal's voice over the loudspeaker. "This is the all clear. Staff and students, you are free to take your things and go home. Those of you taking the bus, you have ten minutes to get on board. Those of you walking or riding your bikes, please stay clear of the fire trucks and be safe. Please clear the halls. This is the all clear. We'll see you tomorrow for our regular Tuesday schedule."

"Finally, and we don't have to wait for anyone!" Aria burst out and jumped to her feet. "I'm out of here."

Madalyn, Wendy, and Natalie got to their feet as well, following Aria to the giant line of students waiting to squeeze out the gymnasium doors and into the hallway.

Madalyn listened to the voices around her, arguing, exclaiming, and complaining about how long it was taking.

Wendy wondered, "Well, what are we supposed to do about homework?"

Aria snorted. "Of *course* you're worried about homework."

"I'm not worried, I'm just asking!"

Everyone was surging toward the doors, and suddenly, Natalie was beside her.

"Um, Madalyn? I have to use the bathroom. Will you wait and walk home with me?"

Why? Madalyn thought, but she forced a smile. "Um, if you want. I'll be by the office."

"Thanks! I'll be quick!" Natalie said, and took off down the hall.

It took a few minutes, but Madalyn wasn't in any rush to get to the other end of the hall. She moved slowly through the crowds of hurrying students and leaned against the wall by the office to wait. From where she stood, she could see lines of cars slowing to peer through the murky air, and the nose-stinging reek of blackened grass was even stronger than before. It made Madalyn a little sad that she couldn't really see the flowering bushes and pretty green lawn through the window. Everything was shades of gray.

"Ready?" Natalie asked, hitching her bag up higher and pulling out a pair of heart-shaped sunglasses.

"Ready," Madalyn said, wishing she had her visor. Outside it was hot, and the wind whirled hot air into her face and into her hair. Ugh. Sometimes Miss Peach walked around with a big, black umbrella when it was hot outside. Madalyn wished she had one. The sun was a tiny, angry orange ball in the sky, and the air felt like a furnace, trying to melt her skin.

The two of them walked down the ramp to the sidewalk, and Madalyn blinked as her eyes started to sting. There was ash in the air, and Madalyn was grateful the school wasn't any closer to where the fire had come; it smelled *horrible*. Natalie pulled her headband out of her hair and wrapped it around her nose. Madalyn wished she had a headband, too. She pulled the collar of her T-shirt up over her face and hurried on.

Madalyn unlocked her bike from the rack, and the two girls walked with it between them. A single fire truck and a few cars from the sheriff's department were still hanging around, directing the cars to move carefully and helping students cross the road safely. Madalyn looked at the students by the high school, who were mostly walking around with their shirts over their faces too, heading for home like the junior high students. There would be no football or tennis practice outside today.

With the sheriff's deputy acting as a crossing guard, Madalyn and Natalie crossed the street and passed the library where several little kids stood inside, faces pressed against the glass, watching the kids walk by. Madalyn wiggled her fingers at a few of the tiniest babies, but Natalie didn't wave or speak. She just kept sniffling into her headband and sneezing. Finally, they made it to the corner of Gatland Street and turned away from all the extra cars and people. They didn't turn away from the awful smell of smoke, though. It swirled in the air and made the sky a dirty whitish-gray color. Madalyn rubbed her face, feeling her eyes tearing as they tried to remove the stinging ash. She sure hoped Papa Lobo had closed all the windows. She hated this awful, choking smell.

They were almost to the house when Natalie seemed to wake up. She looked around the street, at the willow tree in the yard of the house on the corner and the noisy squirrel chattering on the power line above them. "I don't usually come this way," she said, her voice a little foggy and hoarse from the smoke. "We live in a townhouse on Foothill Road, so I usually go straight up Gatland. This way is quieter."

"I only know one way to go." Madalyn shrugged. "I'm just glad I have my bike."

"I should ride my bike, too," Natalie said. "Mostly I walk to the library, and Annica picks me up from there."

"I could do that sometime," Madalyn said. "And . . ." She swallowed. "Maybe sometimes you could come over to our house, too. I mean—if you want."

"Um, I, uh, can't," Natalie said, looking embarrassed.

"Not *now*," Madalyn said. "But once your sister meets Papa Lobo, then you can, right? If you want to go to the library first, fine. We can read in my room."

Natalie's smile clouded over. "That's okay. Um, sometimes Annica doesn't get home until really late, like after I go to bed. She likes me to be home."

Madalyn opened her mouth to answer when she saw Papa Lobo leaning out the front door. She waved, grinning as he waved back, a coffee mug gripped in his other hand. "Ey, *mamzèl*, thought I was gonna have to haul you on out of there!"

Madalyn shrugged. "I know! We had a fire," she hollered back.

"Heard the sirens before the school sent me the text." Papa Lobo took a sip of coffee as Jean appeared in the doorway behind him. Madalyn was briefly indignant—how did he always get out of school before she did?—then ignored him in favor of Papa Lobo's question.

"Who's your little friend?"

"This is Natalie," Madalyn called back.

"Hey, Miss Natalie," Papa Lobo boomed back, and waved like she was a long-lost niece.

Natalie's wave was stiff, and her face was blotchy pink. "Madalyn, I'll talk to you tomorrow," she mumbled, and hurried to cross the street.

"Wait," Madalyn complained, following a few steps. "Not yet! Can't you sit on the porch and have a soda? Or just—sit?"

Natalie, walking backward, shook her head, darting a quick glance at Papa Lobo and Jean. She gave a delicate little cough. "The air—it's making me sick. I'd better just go home."

"Didn't you want me to walk you home?" Madalyn asked, exasperated. What was going on? That cough was totally fake—Natalie hadn't coughed once until now, and she still had her bandanna tied across her nose. Was she *still* afraid of Jean, after all this time? Or was it something else now?

"It's only two more blocks." Natalie shrugged, shifting her weight uncomfortably. She looked like she wanted to hurry away. "I just . . . I didn't want to be nosy, but I wanted to see where you live. You have a nice house."

"Well . . . thanks, but it's Papa Lobo's," Madalyn said, frowning a little. "If you still want to see, maybe next time you can come up to my room? You can ask your sister first, right?"

"Maybe," Natalie said politely, taking another step back toward the opposite sidewalk.

"Well, okay . . ." Madalyn racked her brain for something else friendly to say. "You have my number, right? You can text me, if Annica is late, or if you want. Or whatever."

Natalie's smile was a little more real this time. "Okay."

Madalyn propped her foot on the bike pedal closest to her and pressed down, rolling the bike a little way forward. She wiped sweat from her forehead. "Natalie . . . Are you *sure* you can't stop, just for one more minute? Last night, Jean brought over ice-cream sandwiches. I can go grab some if he didn't pig it all up, and—"

Natalie shook her head hard, her long hair swinging emphatically. "*No. I can't.* I—Annica said I should stay away from boys like that," she said, her voice almost a whisper.

Madalyn froze, her foot suspended on the bike pedal. She opened her mouth, snapped it shut, then opened it again. This was just like the awful morning the first week of school when Aria and Wendy had talked to her. "Boys like . . . *what?*" she managed, feeling her throat tighten.

"You know, like—" Natalie started to say something, then looked away, her long hair forming a curtain that hid her face. She shrugged a shoulder. "Never mind."

Inside Madalyn, it almost seemed like something pulled, then cracked with an awful, cold snap. She swallowed, hard. Jaw tight, she pushed her bike up the sidewalk, across the driveway, and toward the side gate.

"Wait! Wait, Madalyn—" Natalie began, but Madalyn shook her head once, hard. Her hands were cold and her chin was shaking, and she was very careful to keep her eyes stretched open wide and to blink hard.

Papa Lobo, who had been poking at Jean and was

about to follow him back inside, frowned down at Madalyn from the porch. He looked across the street at Natalie and back to Madalyn again. "Your little friend not coming inside, *ché*?"

Madalyn's voice sounded like a scrape of rocks and gravel. "I don't think she's my friend."

Twisting in the Wind

Madalyn bent to put her sherbet bowl into the dishwasher and blinked hard as her gaze drifted upward toward the window. The dull gray sky was an orange-and-yellow smear along the horizon, and the plunging sun was now an angry red. She shivered. It looked super creepy and wrong.

Madalyn pulled out her phone and snapped a picture. **Spooky,** she texted, and sent it to Avery.

Ugh! Avery texted back. **Too smoky here to see the sky.**

Madalyn sighed and went back to her room. There was too much bad news. Mom was so busy at work she couldn't talk to her when she called. Avery and her family had to leave their nice new house in Winters and move to a hotel away from the fires because the smoke made Antony wheeze so badly, they were afraid he'd have to go to the hospital. And Natalie—Madalyn shut down that thought.

Papa Lobo put dinner on the table after Jean went home, and they spent the meal listening to the news on the radio while they ate. After one story, Papa Lobo got up and pulled out a little TV from the corner cabinet in the kitchen and turned up the news broadcast while they finished up and cleared away the dishes. By the time the dishes were clean, the TV volume was so loud that Madalyn could hear everything the announcer said even with her door closed.

There were fires in the north in Somerset, Dry Creek, Woodland, Sutter, and Piñon City. There were more fires to the south, too—Bardsdale and Santa Jacinta. The Santa Ana winds, named after the deep Santa Ana Canyon on the southern end of California, were blowing hot, dry air toward the coast, and driving little sparks of fire into big blazes that raced over grass and trees and fields. The broadcaster reported that people were being forced to evacuate—to leave their homes for safer areas where they could get a hotel, like Avery's family, or stay with friends. The weather forecast said that the hot, dry weather would continue—and so would the wind.

Madalyn heard Papa Lobo mutter something, and then the back door closed with a bang.

Distracted and restless, Madalyn wandered out of her bedroom into the kitchen in time to see Papa Lobo come back into the house a moment later carrying a flat, white paper square.

"What's that?" Madalyn asked as Papa Lobo crouched in the front hallway and took a screwdriver out of his back pocket.

"Air filter," Papa Lobo said, unscrewing a panel near the floor. He reached into the space in the wall and pulled out a dingy paper square and leaned it against the corner. "With all this smoke, got to make sure we've got good air," he said, replacing the filter and carefully screwing on the panel again.

"Eew!" Madalyn examined the dirty filter, making a face at the dust caked onto the filter material. "That's kind of gross."

"Filter's doing its job. There's a lot of smoke in the air," Papa Lobo said, slowly getting to his feet. His knees popped. "We'll keep the air on, and the windows closed, and keep our lungs in good shape," he said, picking up the dirty filter between his first finger and thumb. "Probably oughta hold off pulling any more of that wallpaper—just till we can open up the windows again." He peered at Madalyn. "You best take a look at the school website, see if you have class tomorrow."

Madalyn blinked. "They'll cancel school? Even if there's no fire?"

"Air quality gets bad, gotta close down everything," Papa Lobo said, going back into the kitchen. "Better check."

Madalyn eagerly pulled up the school website on her phone, but the announcement page didn't say anything about fires or air quality or anything. There was just the usual Kingsbridge Junior High logo—a big *K* on a shield surrounded by little twigs of eucalyptus— and a link for the Pegasus log-in page, the school's message board. Madalyn scrolled down, and there was some stuff about a parent survey, and district-wide announcements about the Bay Area Science Olympiad. Madalyn wasn't sure if she was disappointed or relieved that there was nothing new.

Trying to do homework at the sturdy desk in her room, Madalyn couldn't focus. She tried to lay out her outfit for the next day—a thin T-shirt and shorts—then decided to wear her T-shirt dress with the happy yellow sunflowers. But somehow the dress looked dumb, and Madalyn didn't want to wear her sparkly flats—what if Natalie wore hers?—so she switched back to shorts again. Aria sent her a picture of her abuela's *pan dulce*, the sweet bread she was eating, which looked so good Madalyn got up and made a piece of cinnamon toast, all crispy with butter and sugar, which she then abandoned after a couple of bites. Twitchy and exhausted, Madalyn was relieved when it was time to wrap her hair and get ready for bed.

"Even though I miss you, I'm glad you're not here," Mom said during their usual bedtime 2Face call. "There's so much smoke that we can't see the hills now. I can barely see the stop sign on the corner." She cleared her throat, frowning. "The air's so dry, I've been drinking ice water ever since I got home. And can you believe the power company announced it's going to turn off the electricity again? They say the wind is so high it might break the wires and cause another fire. I had enough of this last summer."

"Oh, Mom," Madalyn said, feeling guilty at her mother's hoarse voice and tired face. Without power, there would be no air conditioner, no air filter, and smoke . . . seeping inside where it could damage her lungs. Without power, some cell phones wouldn't even work. Madalyn rubbed her chest. "If you don't even have lights or AC, won't your boss let you stay home from work? Can't you come up here?"

"Nah." Mom sighed. "Social workers can't do that. There are too many people who need us. We have so many clients to see that probably even if one of us is on fire, we're going to need to keep going."

Madalyn rolled her eyes but laughed at her mother's silliness, just as she'd intended. "I don't know, if you're on fire, it might make your paperwork easier to deal with," she teased.

"Hah," Mom said. "I doubt it, it's still on my laptop. That's enough about me, though. How was your day?"

Madalyn hesitated, looking away. She wanted to talk, but she'd already been cranky with Mom, and right now, she sounded so tired. "Uh . . . it was okay," she hedged.

But Mom leaned forward, frowning into her phone's camera. "'Uh, okay'? That doesn't sound good. How's Natalie?"

"Horrible," Madalyn blurted, then, unable to keep the words back, "she's horrible, and mean, and awful. I think I hate her."

"What?" Mom's eyes widened, startled. "Babe, what happened?"

And then the story tumbled out. Madalyn added,

swiping her eyes angrily, "I've been trying to do what you said—to listen to her and let her talk, and you said I don't have to agree with her, but she acted racist, Mom. Like Jean wasn't a good person because her sister said so."

"Oh, Madalyn." Mom sighed, rubbing her forehead. "I'm so sorry. Hearing racist words feels like getting punched in the stomach every single time, doesn't it." It wasn't a question. "It's even worse when it comes from someone you hoped was becoming a friend."

"If she thinks all Black boys are 'boys like that,' then she can't be my friend," Madalyn said, and swallowed hard. "Her sister won't ever let her come over—and she probably thinks bad things about Papa Lobo, too."

"Maybe," Mom said. "And Natalie probably has a lot of leftover fear from being bullied, even without her sister's help. Sometimes we find out who people really are when they're scared. So, Madalyn . . . what are you going to do?"

"Do?" Madalyn blurted in disbelief. "There's nothing to do. Natalie's not my friend." She sighed, trying to find a way to make her mother understand. "It's like—remember your favorite weather lady on channel five? The really happy one?"

Mom raised her eyebrows as she tipped back the

last of her water. "Of course. Roberta Gonzalez!"

Madalyn nodded. "Right. She said this weird thing when it might rain, but it might not . . . um, variable clouds? Scattered sunny? Partly cloudy? Something completely random like that, when she could have just said, '*Duh*, there are clouds practically on your head, it's gonna rain.'"

Mom looked amused but mystified. "So, Natalie's like clouds on your head?"

Madalyn rolled her eyes. "*No!* But she might as well be. She's just like . . . only a variable friend. Sometimes she's fine. The rest of the time, she's partly cloudy or whatever, and I can't figure her out."

Mom was nodding, looking proud of Madalyn's weather metaphor. "I like that, babe. But, you know, you could look at it from the other direction. . . . What if you thought of Natalie as partly sunny? Most of the time with most people, there's a chance of things going either way, toward clouds or toward sun." She paused, fishing an ice cube out of her glass.

Madalyn shrugged. "I guess."

"It's a good metaphor for friendship," Mom said, standing up and moving out of camera range for a moment. Madalyn heard a rustling, clinking noise as her mother rummaged in the freezer. "There's a chance that on any day, a friend can take you toward the clouds or the sun," she said, reappearing with her glass topped full of ice and water again. "Remember when you were younger? Sometimes you and Avery got on each other's last nerve and brought out the worst in each other."

Madalyn's brows snapped into a scowl. "Yeah, but that's not the same thing as Nat—"

"I know, I know," Mom interrupted. "I just want you to think about this: Does thinking or believing something racist mean that Natalie is a terrible person who is never going to be worth being friends with?"

Madalyn sighed and crossed her arms. "I know what you want me to say," she mumbled.

"Almost everything takes practice," Mom continued quietly. "Even somebody good enough to be in the WNBA has to practice. So, we know 'good' isn't something that stays that way for all time. Good is something people have to work toward to stay that way."

Madalyn shrugged, silent.

"Friendships take practice—failing at being good to each other, apologizing, and trying again. You and Natalie haven't had a lot of time to work on being good at friendship. You're the only Black girl in your class, one of the few Black people in your school, and being around people of color seems like it's something new to Natalie. That's why I asked you what you wanted to do." Mom paused, and then her words came slowly, as if she was thinking carefully about each one. "You have to decide whether it's worth talking this through with your friend and trying again. Is Natalie worth putting in a little friendship practice?"

Madalyn scowled and looked away. "I don't want to talk to her."

Mom nodded. "I hear you. You're not on this earth to explain that Jean, or Papa Lobo, or Daddy, or you, or anyone else Black is a good person. Your job isn't to help anyone learn to not say racist things or act in racist ways. That's her work to do. But . . . I'm asking you because you've told me a lot about Natalie since you started your new school. You've told me about her nails, and her hair, and how much you liked that she has a lot of funny things to say. You told me how you two talked about Sydney and Carlin, and how she listened to you. . . . So, Madalyn, you're the one who has to decide what friendship is worth having a hard conversation. Because that's the real issue, isn't it? You saw something in Natalie that was ugly and scary when she was someone you admired, and now you have to decide what you're going to do about it."

Madalyn put her hand over her forehead and tried to squeeze away the headache. "But I don't know what to do," she groaned, sounding desperate even to herself. "Why can't you tell me?"

"That's not my job right now," Mom said, smiling sympathetically.

Madalyn slid down in her chair and thumped her forehead against her desk. This was not a job she wanted at all.

Mom coughed a little and sipped her water. "It's late, babe. You're not going to solve all the problems in the universe in one night. Let's talk about this more in the morning. I want you rested for school tomorrow—your teachers will have you catching up on everything you missed in class today. Don't forget you said you had a Language Arts test coming up."

"Bleh." Madalyn grumped, then sighed, straightening from her slump so she could look into the camera again. "Okay, Mom. Um . . . I hope they don't turn the power off, so you get to sleep with the fan on."

"Me too," Mom said, holding her ice water against her cheek. Her voice had gotten hoarse. "It's ridiculous that it's still so hot. I'm going to go fill up the car with gas, program the coffee maker, and then go straight to bed. You go straight to bed, too, babe. Don't stay up and fuss about this 'til all hours—get some real sleep tonight, all right?"

"Okay," grumbled Madalyn, who might have been planning to stay up a while longer. "I'm going. Good night, Mom."

"Try to have sweet dreams," Mom said with a small smile. "I know this isn't easy, babe, but you'll come through. I know it."

Madalyn tugged up the sheet and blanket from the bottom of the bed where she had kicked them away, and lay still a moment, unsure of what had pulled her from sleep. It was warmish still—Papa Lobo turned off the AC at night—and she wanted the covers because the bed was big, and covers were cuddly, not because she was cold. It was quiet now, and the night was still.

A faint sound from elsewhere in the house seeped under the door, and Madalyn blinked sleepily. It was . . . ringing. Papa Lobo's ancient black telephone was bolted to the kitchen wall, and someone was calling it in the middle of the night. Like Mom and Daddy, Papa Lobo didn't use the landline very much, but he didn't really use his cell phone, either. His friends, when they wanted to see him, walked—or in Doc's case, drove—from their respective houses around the neighborhood. If someone was calling the landline now, when it was dark and the whole neighborhood was sleeping, Papa Lobo must have let his cell phone run out of battery—or else it was an emergency.

Madalyn raised up on her elbow and reached for her phone, squinting as she tilted the face toward her to see the clock. It was 4:15 a.m., and someone was calling Papa Lobo now? Madalyn frowned, tiny tendrils of worry wrapping around her heart.

The house phone rang again, and the sound brought Madalyn struggling out of bed, clutching her cell phone in her hand. She swiped across the screen to find the flashlight function and stumbled into the dark hallway just as Papa Lobo, a bathrobe open over his ribbed white undershirt and pajama pants, snapped on the stove light. He snatched up the receiver and answered, his voice husky with sleep.

"'Lo? Who's this? What, now? Macie? Macie, slow down."

Madalyn's heart felt like it might leap right out of her chest. She lunged into the kitchen, bare feet skidding on the old pine boards, and clutched the sleeve of Papa Lobo's robe, eyes wide.

"Mom? Is that Mom?" she demanded.

Nodding, Papa Lobo placed a quieting hand on Mada-lyn's shoulder. "Okay, now—you get yourself on the road, you hear? Don't take the 12, or the interstate—you'll run into folks coming from Bardsdale. Take the 505 and come up over the hills if you can. God willing you won't have any trouble. Uh-huh. Uh-huh." Papa Lobo looked down at Madalyn, and his eyebrows rum-pled. He thrust the old-fashioned phone at her. "Here."

"Mom?" Madalyn said. She had goose bumps.

"Madalyn!" Mom exclaimed, sounding out of breath. "Okay, babe, listen—everything's fine, all right? I've got a full tank. I'm coming out to Papa Lobo's, and everything is going to be fine."

"What?" Any sense of calm Madalyn might have had evaporated like ice cubes in a heat wave. She gripped the curly wire that came from the receiver. "Mom, why are you coming now? We're three hours away, you're going to be late for work!"

"There was a grass fire off the highway at around six, and it sparked a few bushes on the base of Gold Hill Road," she said, coughing a little. "It's now eight hundred acres, burning out of control, and the hills are going up, too. We got an alert on our phones—they're suggesting everyone in this area pack a bag, just in case."

"Just in case—?" Madalyn repeated, dread coating her stomach.

"Just in case the fire gets too close to the house, and we have to leave," Mom said, then broke off to cough. "I'm not going to wait," she continued, her voice a little breathless. "A lot of people are leaving now, trying to get hotels somewhere else, but I'd rather be with you than stuck in a hotel, if I can help it. I called your daddy, and he's gone to the airport to find a flight home as soon as he can . . . right now there are flights, but the smoke in the air might make it hard—" She broke off. "Who is it?"

"Mom?" Madalyn asked, hearing banging noises in the background. Someone was shouting, and she heard her mother suck in a surprised breath as she opened the door and said something to someone.

Her mother's voice came back, louder and shakier, in Madalyn's ear.

"This is it," Mom said. "We're being evacuated. The fire jumped the highway and has blocked the bridge. I need to go before I can't get out."

"The freeway? What? But fire can't burn roads, can it?" Madalyn exclaimed. "Mom . . ."

"Madalyn, I have to go," Mom repeated. "I—"

"Don't hang up," Madalyn blurted, panicking. "Wait, Mama, don't go yet!"

Madalyn heard the jingle of keys and a slam. Her mother spoke quickly, sounding breathless again. "I have to, babe. Right now, there are a lot of scared people trying to leave, and I'll have to focus on driving. As soon as the traffic clears and I can, I'll call you, all right?"

For a second or two, Madalyn couldn't speak. "Well, be careful!" she said, her voice harsh and almost angry sounding.

"I will. I always am. I'll see you in a few hours," Mom said, sounding calmer than she had before. "I love you so much, Madalyn. Try to go back to sleep."

Was she joking? Madalyn almost laughed, but the sound she made didn't sound like laughing. Papa Lobo put his hand on the back of her head like Daddy sometimes did and squished her against his side as he tugged the phone out of her hand. "Macie? Uh-huh. Go on, then." He said something in Creole, a prayer or something, and then hung up, the receiver making a hollow, clunky sound.

Madalyn shivered, feeling panic climb up her insides and threaten to pull her under. Why hadn't she said anything when Mom said she loved her? Why hadn't she been nicer? What if something bad happened, something like a car crash, or the fire jumped back onto the highway and burned up Mom's car with her in it?

Madalyn struggled to draw in a breath, and her throat made an awful noise.

Why were there so many bad things in the world? People set fires, power lines broke, wind drove sparks that burned grass and trees and houses, neighborhoods and cities. What if Mom drove too close to the fires? What if she didn't have anywhere else to go? What if she got too much smoke? What if something happened to Papa Lobo, and Mom never got to her, either? What if she was all alone in the dark, in the smoke, with fire coming?

Madalyn opened her mouth and tried to get more air.

"Madalyn. Madalyn," Papa Lobo said louder, his voice sharp and loud. "Come sit." Taking her arm, Papa Lobo led Madalyn, stumbling, to his recliner by the back door. She dropped onto the edge of the seat and shivered, even though it wasn't really cold. She could hear the loud, rough sound of her breathing going faster and faster. Papa Lobo vanished for a moment, then reappeared with a blanket from somewhere. He unfolded it over her, and Madalyn shuddered as the soft folds slid over her arms. She sat like a statue as Papa Lobo pulled her phone out of her clenched fist, then settled the blanket all the way around her. He even leaned over and fiddled with the lever on the side to make the back of the chair drop down a little. Madalyn scooted back and rested her face against the blanket. She was a little surprised when Papa Lobo pulled a white handkerchief out of the pocket of his bathrobe and held it up against her face.

"Blow," he ordered, and Madalyn tried to slow down her hitching breaths to blow her nose.

Afterward, Papa Lobo leaned back and looked down at her, his rumpled white eyebrows drawn down over worried dark eyes. "All right now?" he asked.

"All right," Madalyn mumbled, and leaned into his warm side. Poor Papa Lobo looked almost scared—of her. Madalyn tried to sit up straight and stop shivering. But her hands were too shaky, and her legs didn't feel like they would hold her up. "I'm all right," she repeated, even though she wasn't entirely sure that this was true.

"Good, good. I'll just make you a little cocoa," Papa Lobo said, and went to the refrigerator to take out Madalyn's oat milk. "You just set there and rest awhile. Your *mamm* and *popa* will come through just fine."

Madalyn pulled her knees up to her chin and sat in a miserable lump as Papa Lobo hummed at the stove, pouring milk into a small pot and stirring it slowly. Soon the sweet smell of cocoa powder and sugar wafted through the room. Madalyn took a deep, trembling breath.

Just then, Madalyn's phone tinkled out a little song from the table where Papa Lobo had set it.

"Mom!" Madalyn sat bolt upright and struggled out of her blanket nest. She picked up the phone and stopped, blinking at the screen. It wasn't Mom.

"Natalie?"

Smoke Gets in Your Eyes

"Annica didn't come home."

Madalyn heard the words only faintly. Disappointment was such a heavy weight in her lungs that she could barely catch her breath. There was a roaring in her ears, the sound of her own breath and heartbeat so loud it almost drowned out the words. Why was Natalie, and not Mom, calling? Why wasn't it Mom with news that she was away from the fire and safely on her way?

"Sorry I woke you up." Natalie ran the apology out in a single breath, sounding rattled. "But Annica didn't come home. Her phone just rings and rings and doesn't go to voice mail."

Madalyn snapped to attention, clutching her blanket closer. "Oh—"

"She told me she was having dinner and then she was coming home," Natalie blurted, her voice wobbling again. "I tried calling her last night, but it went to voice mail. I fell asleep on the couch, and I woke up, and she still wasn't here. I just called, right now, but the phone only makes this weird noise, and it doesn't go through," Natalie added, her voice climbing to a squeaky pitch. "On the school page it says they're going to announce at seven if we're going to have school, and Annica's not here, and I don't know what to do! I'm sorry it's so early, but . . . you said I could call . . ."

"I—I know." Madalyn chewed her bottom lip, her stomach churning. Maybe Annica had gotten caught last night like Mom had this morning? "Can you call your mom and dad?" she asked.

Natalie made a strange sound. "No," she said, and gave a sharp little laugh. "I never met my father. My mom lives in New Mexico now. She . . . kind of dumped me on Annica when I was eight."

"Oh." Madalyn's stomach swooped. She tried to think what to say. "That's . . . not good."

"So, I can't—" Natalie began, then swallowed loudly. "You said I could call."

But that was before, Madalyn wanted to say. She rubbed her face, remembering what Mom had said, but all she could do was worry. Was Natalie worth having a hard conversation? What if she wasn't? Madalyn didn't know how to have a hard conversation, not right now.

Tilting her phone, Madalyn checked the time, and her shoulders slumped. It wasn't even five yet. Madalyn wished Natalie had called someone else. Where was Mom now? But Natalie was still waiting for her to say something.

"Um . . . do you want to get on 2Face? We can, um, watch some more news at five. Maybe there's something we can find out about Sacramento," Madalyn offered. "Maybe there are lots of people stuck, and nobody can call because they turned the power off. That's what my . . . my mom said they were going to do. Sometimes it makes cell phones not work." Madalyn heard the wobble in her voice now. She looked at the time again. Why hadn't Mom called? Wasn't driving for half an hour enough to be somewhere safe, so she could call?

Natalie sniffled. "I—"

"Drink this down, *mamzèl*," Papa Lobo murmured, setting a fragrant mug of chocolate on the table in front of her. Madalyn jumped. She'd almost forgotten he was in the kitchen.

"It's, um, Natalie," she whispered, gesturing to the phone. "Her sister got stuck . . . somewhere. She didn't come home yesterday, and Natalie's scared."

Papa Lobo passed a hand over Madalyn's hair and shook his head, making a troubled sound. "Poor thing. Let me go put something on—I'll carry her over here in the truck till her folks come home."

Madalyn recoiled. "What? No!" Madalyn covered the phone again and lowered her voice to a sharp whisper. "She can't come over *here*. She's . . . she's fine. She's at her house, so she's safe. There's food and stuff. She's fine."

Papa Lobo's brows jumped so high his forehead wrinkled. "I see."

Her face hot and her stomach churning, Madalyn turned back to her phone call. "Sorry—that was just Papa Lobo," she said. "He, um, brought me hot chocolate."

"I woke him up, too?" Natalie said, sounding horrified. "Are you in trouble?"

"No, I . . . my mom woke us up," Madalyn said, feeling her throat get tight all over again. "She got evacuated. She's trying to get away from the fire."

Natalie gasped. "Oh no! Madalyn!"

Madalyn could feel tears coming all over again. "I—don't," she said, then pressed her fingers over her eyes and cleared her throat. "Never mind. You should make something to drink before the news comes on. Do you have hot chocolate?"

"I think so . . . ," Natalie said. "I'll have to look."

"Go look," Madalyn said. "I'll go to the bathroom, and I'll call you back on 2Face."

Madalyn hung up the phone and struggled out of Papa Lobo's recliner. "Papa Lobo? Papa Lobo!"

Had he gone back to bed? Madalyn dragged her blanket across the room until she stood in the hallway. Her great-uncle emerged from his bedroom, buttoning on one of his deep blue coveralls.

"She *can't* come over here," Madalyn exclaimed. "Remember she wouldn't even come sit on the front porch yesterday? Her sister doesn't like Black people!"

Papa Lobo's eyebrows were still raised. "So?"

Madalyn waved a hand, trying to find the words. "So she might . . . say something. She—I—we aren't friends like that, Papa Lobo."

Papa Lobo shrugged a little and tilted his head. "Don't have to *be* friends to help somebody, do you?"

Madalyn gnawed her lip. "No, but—"

"The time is always right to do what's right," Papa Lobo said. "Always time to be a good neighbor."

"Don't you care that she's acting like a racist?" Madalyn blurted. He didn't know what Natalie had said—and how she'd said it. Papa Lobo *loved* his godson, Jean. If he knew how Natalie was . . .

Papa Lobo pushed his jaw forward and squinted a bit, thinking. "Not too much, no. *Bondyeu* don't give us too much time to be worrying about that. All I've got to see to is how *I'm* going to act, *ché.*"

Madalyn opened her mouth, then closed it, biting her tongue until it hurt. Papa Lobo didn't get it. "She . . . she won't want to come over here."

Papa Lobo stepped out of his room and patted Madalyn on the shoulder as he passed. "Maybe. Maybe not. That's up to her."

Madalyn wavered in the hallway, torn between following him to explain and calling Natalie to prove her point. Sighing, she pushed the button for Natalie's number.

"Hey. So, we have chocolate," Natalie announced, "but it's Annica's diet chocolate, which is gross, so I'm just going to make tea like that Jane Austen book—"

"Papa Lobo made me hot chocolate on the stove with whipped cream," Madalyn said, her voice almost challenging. "He wrapped me up in a blanket when I was freaking out, and he let me sit in his recliner. And he already got dressed so *you* could come over, even though you wouldn't even come sit on his porch."

Natalie drew an audible breath. "I—Madalyn, I can't—"

"I know your sister told you to stay away from Black boys," Madalyn stated. "Well, there are no boys here. There's me, and there's Papa Lobo, and if you don't want to be by yourself, he says he'll come over and pick you up. It's an emergency, and Annica can't get mad."

Natalie was silent.

Madalyn's shoulders slumped. *See?* she felt like telling Papa Lobo. It didn't matter how she'd chosen to act. It didn't matter if people said or did all the right things. People like Natalie and her sister always stayed the same.

Madalyn tilted the phone. It was five o'clock. Mom had been driving for at least a half hour now, and she still hadn't called. Madalyn leaned her head back against the wall and sighed, closing her gritty, tired eyes. She imagined the freeway packed with cars, traffic jammed into every lane as scared people drove away from the smoke and flames as fast as they could.

But Mom wasn't driving fast—she couldn't be, or she would have pulled over somewhere safe to call by now. Was she still in traffic? Had she gotten out of town or had to turn around and go another way?

Where was she?

"Madalyn? Madalyn, what's your address?" Natalie asked again.

"What?" Madalyn had almost forgotten what they were talking about.

"What's your papa's house number on Gatland? I have to write it on a note and tape it on the door, so Annica doesn't freak. I can't leave her a voice mail, so she won't know where I am."

Madalyn's eyes snapped open. "Um . . . it's 209. You're actually . . . you're coming? And you want us to pick you up?"

"Yes, please. Annica likes to meet my friends' parents first," Natalie said, and her voice was resigned. "But the light's all weird and orange, and I only know how to make grilled cheese, and . . . I don't want to be by myself anymore."

"I—well, okay then," Madalyn said, a little dazed. "Tell me your address, and we'll be right there."

A Breaking Storm

The *tick-tick-tick* of the turn signal was the loudest thing in Papa Lobo's truck, although Madalyn was sure her heart was at least as loud. Natalie had been waiting on the sidewalk in front of the townhouse and before Papa Lobo had even put the truck in park, she'd shouldered her bag and hurried over, holding the neck of her T-shirt over her nose.

"Hey," Madalyn said, opening the door and scooting to the middle seat.

"Hey," Natalie said, holding up a striped duffel bag. "Should I put this in back?"

"No, there's room," Madalyn said. "Hop in."

"Good morning, Miss Natalie," Papa Lobo said with

his usual sunshiny smile.

"Thanks for picking me up, um, Mr. Lobo," Natalie said, giving Papa Lobo a nervous glance.

"It's actually Mr. Thomas," Madalyn said, then felt bad at Natalie's embarrassed wince.

"Don't worry about it. Mr. Lobo is fine." Papa Lobo smiled and turned the truck around.

And now the truck was dead quiet as they rolled through the dark streets. Natalie was twisting the long braid of her hair, staring at nothing. Madalyn was picking at the stitching on her seat belt, wondering what she'd gotten herself into. She and Natalie should talk about things, but Madalyn wasn't sure how—or when. What could she say? And when was the right time to say, "I think maybe you were being racist, and I didn't like it"? What if Natalie didn't understand?

"Looks like Father Andreas is up," Papa Lobo said, nodding toward a tall building.

Madalyn leaned forward and looked toward the church, which, except for the parking lot, was mostly a dark outline at this hour, but it had light shining from the small stained-glass windows running up its center. "There's services now?"

"Some folks like to get in there early. Lots to pray about today," Papa Lobo said.

Madalyn nodded and touched the phone in her pocket, a silent prayer of her own.

All too soon, Papa Lobo was backing the truck into its usual spot in the driveway.

Papa Lobo opened the front door and smiled. "You make yourself at home, Miss Natalie. I'm just going to put some coffee on and scramble up some breakfast. I'll holler for you when it's done."

"Thanks," Madalyn said, and turned to Natalie, who was examining the front hallway as if she'd never seen one before. "Come put your bag in my room." Madalyn invited her, and Natalie nodded.

Madalyn walked slowly, looking at the glass panels in the front room doors, the slightly shiny wallpaper, and the clock ticking quietly beneath its glass dome on the entryway hall table. It was strange to imagine Papa Lobo's house through someone else's eyes. To Natalie, the hallway probably seemed narrow and dark, and full of weird smells like old houses got. Madalyn wished now that she had made her bed before having Natalie over, but she hadn't even taken the time to take off her sleep scarf and brush out her hair. She hoped Natalie wouldn't think—

A double knock on the front door introduced the sound of the knob turning. Madalyn winced, expecting

Jean, and drew back a little as a tall figure wearing a hoodie and a bandanna across the lower half of her face stepped inside.

Natalie took a step back. "Who's that?" she whispered.

"You in there, old man?" a woman's voice called, and then she pulled her bandanna down. "Good morning, ladies. One of you must be Madalyn."

Madalyn snapped out of her surprise. "Um, that's me," she said, disentangling herself from Natalie's grip and taking a hesitant step toward the tall, brown-skinned woman with the crooked smile that looked like Jean's. "This is my friend Natalie—and you're the one who gave me those sunflowers, right, Mrs. Duval?"

Jean's mother beamed as Papa Lobo came out of the kitchen. "Yes, I am—I'm so glad you enjoyed them. Good morning, old man, I saw your truck pulling in, and I wanted to make sure everything was okay. I'm just headed out for a little exercise."

"We're just fine, but you best stay here and have some coffee—too much smoke out there for all that running around," Papa Lobo said.

"I just might, at that," Mrs. Duval said, moving past Madalyn with a friendly smile and following Papa Lobo. "I'm pretty sure I won't have students today—I guess I've got a minute or two."

The two adults continued, chatting, into the kitchen. Madalyn turned back to Natalie with an awkward smile. "So, that's our neighbor—" she began.

"You guys don't lock the door?" Natalie whispered, her brows raised. "What if a robber walked in or something?"

Madalyn grinned. "Mrs. Duval isn't a robber, and she probably has a key. She teaches biology at the high school. Friends of Papa Lobo are pretty much family." Madalyn turned to lead the way toward her bedroom, adding over her shoulder, "Anyway, Papa Lobo says if anyone can find anything worth stealing in this old house, they're welcome to it."

"Well, we *always* lock up our townhouse," Natalie announced. "Annica says you can't be too careful these days."

Madalyn grimaced as she opened her bedroom door. She didn't want to talk about Annica, but maybe this was a good opening? Madalyn swallowed. "Listen, Natalie? I—"

"Wow, this is your room? It's huge! I love your curtains," Natalie interrupted, standing in the doorway and looking around.

Madalyn backed toward her bed and sat, tucking up

her legs as Natalie peeped into her closet, looked out her window, and examined the picture frames on her dresser. "It's one of Papa Lobo's guest rooms," Madalyn said, looking at the black-and-white throw rug that matched the plain white metal bedframe, "but I like it. This is way bigger than my room at home."

"Mine too," Natalie said. She dragged her finger over the stack of library books on Madalyn's desk. "You read a lot, huh?"

"Yep," Madalyn said. "You should read one of those—the TBH novels are all written in text messages, and they're really funny."

"Maybe later," Natalie said, and sank down into the big cushy chair by the window. "I brought all my polish and stuff, if you want to do your nails."

"Oh, um, thanks." Madalyn glanced at Natalie's bag, where it sat on the floor next to her bedroom door. "Maybe later. Do you, um, want to make some earrings? I have embroidery thread that matches your nail polish."

"Oh! Yeah! We should do that later." Natalie fiddled with her hair, then twisted the length of it around her fingers. An awkward silence fell. Madalyn opened her mouth—then closed it again. She wished she weren't so afraid to say the wrong thing. Madalyn really wanted Natalie to be her friend, but they still had to have their hard talk first.

Well, maybe not right now.

"So, are you hungry?" Madalyn asked, bouncing to her feet. "Papa Lobo's making eggs—or, we have sourdough, so you can have avocado toast."

"Um . . . maybe later," Natalie said again. "I-Is it okay if I stay in here for a minute?"

Madalyn blinked. "Stay here? You mean, by yourself?"

Natalie twisted her hands together. "I won't touch anything. I just . . . I want to try calling my sister again."

Madalyn understood immediately, though her stomach twisted. She wished she could call Mom, but she didn't dare. What if she was driving and Madalyn's call distracted her? Madalyn swallowed and clenched her fingers around her phone. "Sure," she said, shoving the phone into the pocket of her shorts. "If you need the bathroom, it's next door, that way," she said, and pointed to the right. "And I'll be in the kitchen—that's the yellow room, straight down the hall."

"Thanks," Natalie said, swiping her finger over the screen to wake her phone.

Papa Lobo was chatting with Mrs. Duval and

whipping the eggs when Madalyn came in. The air smelled like coffee and toast, which made Madalyn's stomach growl. It felt strange to be hungry—normally she would be just waking up now.

Madalyn found her mug of hot chocolate on the table where she'd left it and put it back into the microwave to warm. She sighed, watching the mug turn circles through the little window. She wished Mom would call. Even if she didn't get to ask her mother about talking to Natalie, Madalyn just wanted more than anything to hear her voice.

Hard conversations were supposed to be hard. But if Natalie was right in Madalyn's room, the kind of conversation they needed to have felt impossible. How did people do it? And who showed them how?

"Got some toast for you," Papa Lobo said, and put a plate on the table. "Where's your little friend?"

Madalyn retrieved her mug of chocolate and sat at the table. "Natalie's trying to call her sister again," she said, hunching over the sweet-smelling drink.

"Poor child," Papa Lobo said quietly. "How are you holding up, *mamzél*?"

Madalyn opened her mouth to say she was fine but had to swallow hard before she could say anything. She was grateful that Papa Lobo hadn't forgotten that she was worried and scared, too. Since Mom hadn't called, Madalyn knew she wasn't safe yet. After another hour, Madalyn wasn't sure she would be holding up for very much longer, but for right now . . .

"I'm all right," Madalyn said, her voice rough. She cleared her throat. She hadn't been the only one woken up and worried. "Are you all right, Papa Lobo?"

Setting a plate of sliced oranges on the table, Papa Lobo gave her a fond smile. "This old man is just fine, *ché*."

Mrs. Duval smiled, too, about to say something when Madalyn's phone buzzed. Eagerly Madalyn opened her messages and sighed at the message from the unfamiliar number. Not Mom, but the Highland County School District.

Madalyn held up the phone. "You were right, Papa Lobo. No school," she confirmed.

"Good," Papa Lobo said. "None of you kids need to be breathing all that smoke."

"No school for you, but teachers still have to at least check in," Mrs. Duval sighed, standing. "I'd better go get myself together. Thanks for the coffee, Lo. I'm sure I'll see you all later. Madalyn, have a good day."

Madalyn waved and got up to get Natalie as Papa Lobo put the finishing touches on breakfast.

Madalyn tapped at the door. "Natalie? Are you still on the phone?"

"No." Madalyn heard a deep sniffle and opened the door a little.

"She still didn't answer?"

"No." Natalie was curled up miserably in Madalyn's comfortable chair. Her eyelids were pink, and her face was blotchy and damp. "The phone is still making that weird beeping. And there's no school, either."

"I know. I got the text." Madalyn hovered awkwardly in the doorway. She didn't know what else to say. "Papa Lobo made breakfast."

Natalie shook her head. "I'm not hungry."

Madalyn fidgeted. If it were Avery feeling sick and sad, she'd know what to do, but somehow Madalyn knew all the things that would work for Avery—giving her a hug, getting Papa Lobo to reassure her—wouldn't make Natalie feel any better. "Um . . . okay. I'll ask Papa Lobo to make you some chocolate."

Natalie shook her head. "No, thank you. I don't . . . I don't want to bother him."

"You're not." Madalyn hesitated, then took the blanket folded across the bottom of her bed and shook it open. "If you cuddle up in this for a while you might go back to sleep. This is a good chair for naps."

Natalie sniffled a little and took the blanket. "Thanks."

Madalyn backed into the hallway and closed the door.

Back in the kitchen, Madalyn sat down at the scarred wooden table. Papa Lobo, who was reading the paper while the TV news played in the background, looked around curiously as Madalyn served herself some eggs, toast, and fruit. She was shaking hot sauce onto her eggs before Papa Lobo said anything.

"Miss Natalie not hungry?" Papa Lobo asked.

"She's feeling kind of bad." Madalyn sighed. "She still can't get hold of her sister. I gave her a blanket so she could maybe go to sleep or something."

"You make her up a little plate for later, then," Papa Lobo said, and frowned. "She doesn't have any other folks 'round here? Where's her mama and daddy?"

Madalyn shrugged. "Her mom moved. She lives with her sister."

Papa Lobo shook his head and got up. "I'll make some more cocoa," he said.

Madalyn smiled to herself. Papa Lobo really believed hot chocolate could fix anything.

Madalyn had just taken another bite of eggs when the black kitchen telephone gave its loud ring.

Before Papa Lobo had turned halfway toward the phone, Madalyn was already up on her feet, practically vibrating in place. "Papa Lobo?"

Papa Lobo jerked his chin toward the phone. "Whatcha waiting on?"

Madalyn darted toward the phone and the heavy black handset, her throat dry. "Thomas residence."

"Madalyn!"

"Daddy! Where are you? Have you heard from Mom? Is she okay?" Madalyn blurted the questions in quick succession. "Are you okay?"

"I'm okay, babe," Daddy said, sounding rushed. "I'm at the airport in Phoenix—they just canceled all flights into the Bay Area. I'm going to take a commuter flight into LA or San Jose and see if I can rent a car, but I won't get up there till this afternoon, late. Where's the old man?"

"He's right here," Madalyn said, turning toward Papa Lobo, who was hovering over her shoulder. Papa Lobo reached for the phone, but Madalyn held up her finger. "Daddy—have you heard from Mom?"

"Not since early this morning, but I'm sure she's fine," Daddy said, and Madalyn heard impatience in his voice. "I left her a message. She's smart and she's not going to take any risks, and she'll call us when she's safe. Let me talk to Uncle Lobo, babe."

Madalyn held out the phone to her great-uncle and leaned against the wall, trying to listen in to what her father said. Papa Lobo looked serious and said "Mm-hmm" a lot, and Madalyn thought of what her father had said.

Daddy might be sure that Mom was fine, but Madalyn wasn't. Smart didn't stop fires from jumping across a road and igniting grass on the other side. Smart didn't stop smoke from being thick and hard to see through. Sometimes being smart wasn't any match for being in danger.

Madalyn rubbed her arms. If she were smart, she'd finish her breakfast, but it felt like her stomach was twisted metal. Swallowing, Madalyn picked up her plate and set it on the counter. Now she was too worried to eat, too.

Foul Weather Friend

Papa Lobo had a coffee cup with a big-headed fisherman on it, being pulled into the water by an even bigger-headed fish. The words "Tough times never last, but tough people do" were written in blue on its smooth tan sides. Madalyn liked the silly-looking fish (and wondered who was supposed to be having the tough time—the fish or the fisherman) but she liked the words on the mug best of all. The words would be a nice thing to hear if you were having a bad time. "It won't last, but you will." It might not always be true, but she really hoped it was—especially now.

Madalyn sighed and leaned her forehead against the front room window. It was warm against her skin, contrasting with the cool air whispering from the metal vent beneath her feet. Outside it was dim and dark, like the worst sort of foggy day, and the trees moved restlessly in the constant wind. It was almost ten o'clock, and Mom still hadn't called—nor could Madalyn call her. She'd tried. Twice.

Even Daddy's phone had gone straight to voice mail. Maybe he was still on a plane. Maybe he was driving somewhere. The morning news had reports about public safety power outages causing cell phone problems, just like Mom had said. People were unable to get calls or call out, because the power company's blackouts had included cell phone towers. People were advised to listen to radios that used batteries if they had them. Papa Lobo had asked Madalyn to help him make a grocery list so he could make sure they had something that Natalie would like to eat when she woke up—and he'd added batteries as the very first thing on the list, just in case.

Madalyn moved her forehead from the glass and rubbed away the smudge it left. Twenty minutes ago, Papa Lobo had pulled on his ball cap, wrapped a blue bandanna around his nose like a bandit, and drove off. And with Natalie still asleep and the TV full of nothing but morning talk shows and cartoons, Madalyn couldn't stop her brain from going in circles.

She'd wandered the house, peeping into Papa Lobo's room, which smelled strongly of his soap, poking through the other small guest room, and finally Madalyn had wound up in the front room, standing in the midst of newspapers and boxes Papa Lobo had set aside to wrap up the roosters. There was still a lot to do to finish the room. The wood paneling had left hundreds of tiny nail holes that needed to be filled and sanded flat; the roosters needed to be wrapped in newspaper, boxed, and carried to the attic; the remaining wood panels needed to be carted outside; and then there was washing the walls and painting. Madalyn had stood in the front room for ten minutes, intending to get started on *something*, but she just hadn't found the energy.

Madalyn pulled out her phone and swiped her thumb across the screen. She pressed the button that would connect her to Mom's cell phone and bit her bottom lip as the line rang and rang and rang.

After two minutes of listening to the phone ring, Madalyn hung up and thunked her head against the window again. Now that she knew Mom probably couldn't call her, either, Madalyn didn't feel any better. Somehow, that made everything worse.

Madalyn was dragging herself away from the window when she spied activity across the street. Mrs. Baylor—nearly dwarfed by another huge hat—was out in her yard with . . . a basket? She was cutting plants or something. Madalyn winced as the old woman straightened from cutting something and coughed. Mrs. Baylor obviously loved her garden, but there was definitely too much smoke in the air for yard work. The lady on the news said that everyone was supposed to stay indoors and avoid doing things that didn't absolutely need to be done, like exercising and running around. Even the gray cat had sense enough to stay inside and not pester anyone today.

Papa Lobo's truck turned up the street, followed by a long white car cruising along behind. Madalyn's heart lifted. That was Doc, Papa Lobo's friend, driving the giant car Jean had nicknamed "Moby." Madalyn liked Doc. He'd brought her a mini candy bar and a comic cut from the newspaper the first time they'd met.

She watched as Papa Lobo got out with his groceries and Doc got out of his car, a newspaper tucked under his arm. He crossed to the middle of the road to say something to Mrs. Baylor, who said something back—waving her finger—then coughed into her elbow. She glared after the men as Doc and Papa Lobo shook their heads and turned back toward the house.

"—can't make no kind of sense of that woman," Papa Lobo was saying as he came in and moved aside for Doc, who moved a bit stiffly, leaning on his cane. "Her sister sure got all the sweetness in that family; Edna Baylor is as contrary as a granite rock."

"Well, you can tell some people something sometimes," Doc said calmly, pulling off the paper mask that covered the bottom half of his face, "but the rest of them you can't tell a darned thing at all, Lo. Good morning, madam."

"Good morning, Dr. Buchannan," Madalyn said, standing in the doorway of the front room. The bitter smoke smell was thick, and she was glad the air was on. "Papa Lobo, do you have the stuff that we're supposed to use to fix the walls?"

"I do," Papa Lobo said. "Let me put this down, and I'll find it." Papa Lobo headed toward the kitchen and called over his shoulder, "C'mon in, Doc. I got some iced tea in here."

Madalyn trailed along behind him, pausing at hearing a noise as she passed the door to her room. She opened the door a crack and laughed as Natalie's head popped up from where she was digging around in her bag.

"Madalyn! Oh my gosh, I am *so* sorry I went to sleep!"

Natalie stood up, looking flustered. Her face was creased with sleep marks and hair straggled out from her fuzzy braid in all directions.

"That's okay—you were probably tired. Are you hungry yet?"

"I'm okay. I was looking for my brush—" Natalie gave her bag an annoyed look and shook her head. "I'll have to find it later. Where's the bathroom again?"

Madalyn took advantage of Natalie stepping out to quickly pull the covers up on her bed and put on something she hadn't slept in. She combed her own hair and was pulling it back into a low ponytail when Natalie came back. The hair around Natalie's face was wet, and she looked a little more awake.

"Thank you for the chocolate you left me," Natalie said, looking shy. "It was really good, even cold."

"You're welcome. We can go in the kitchen and make more. Papa Lobo is probably still in there. He makes the cocoa from scratch."

Natalie unraveled her braid all the way and brushed the ends to detangle it. "I'm okay for now, but maybe later." She gave Madalyn a hesitant look. "Have you . . . Did your mom call?"

"No." Madalyn swallowed. "I talked to my dad . . . before he got on his plane, but . . ." Madalyn swallowed again. "Nothing." Madalyn winced saying that last word, then tried hard to turn it sunnier, brighter, like Mom would. "It's just the phones, probably. The news says a lot of them aren't working right now, so . . ."

"Right," Natalie said, nodding. "I saw that online. So that's probably it—she just can't call you because of the phone. But she's probably tried—just like we tried calling, too."

Madalyn shivered and rubbed her arms. "Yeah."

Both girls turned toward the door at a commotion in the hallway. "*Paren*, where y'at?" Madalyn heard Jean yell and rolled her eyes. Could he not just come into a house quietly, like a normal person?

"Who . . . is that—" Natalie's eyes were wide.

Oh no. Madalyn stepped back quickly and closed her bedroom door, hoping Natalie wasn't about to get weird again. "Um, that's Jean, from down the street— Mrs. Duval's son. Look, Natalie—I know you got bullied by a Black boy, but Jean's not a bully, I promise. He's kind of annoying, but he's not mean, okay? I swear it. And if he is? We'll get him in trouble with Papa Lobo *and* his mom."

Natalie shot a glance at the door and spoke almost

in a whisper. "Um . . . actually. I need to tell you something, Madalyn, and don't get mad, but . . . I told Annica about you."

"Okay," Madalyn said, confused. "Told her what?"

"Just about how you're always so nice to me, and you're good at math, and that you invited me over." Natalie swallowed. "Annica said she didn't have time to meet anyone's parents, but she was glad I was making friends, and it was, um, okay with her if we hung out sometimes."

Natalie said the last part in a rushed mutter, and Madalyn's eyes widened. "Wait, what?"

"I was coming over yesterday, but then I saw that boy and I got nervous, and—and I wanted to tell you the truth before Annica got here. I'm sorry. Okay?"

Madalyn blinked, then blinked again. *Okay?* She thought this was okay? "You *lied*? Why did you lie?"

Natalie grimaced. "I was nervous. I didn't mean to—"

"What do you mean, you didn't mean to?" Madalyn blazed. "You told me Annica said not to be around boys like Jean. I thought she was mean! I thought she was acting racist!"

"She's not!" Natalie exclaimed. "I just—after last year, she said to be careful about being friends with boys. She could have meant a boy like Jean!" At Madalyn's angry look, Natalie continued. "I—you asked me to come over, and then he was here, and I just got scared, so it was easier to tell you that Annica said no, so you wouldn't"—Natalie gulped, and her voice got much quieter—"so you wouldn't get mad at me and not want to be my friend. For saying no."

"Huh. Well, now I'm mad at you for lying." Madalyn's face was hot, and for some reason, her eyes stung. She wanted to cry. She'd been so worried that Annica would be mad—that Natalie would get in trouble for being at Papa Lobo's house—and that Annica would yell, and that she wouldn't want Natalie and Madalyn to be friends. She couldn't believe that Papa Lobo had been so kind—he'd gone to pick Natalie up and cooked special food—for someone like Natalie, who wasn't even *nice*. Madalyn struggled to say all that she felt, but all she could manage was, "I can't *believe* you! You drank Papa Lobo's chocolate and everything!"

"Miss Madalyn!" Papa Lobo's call came a moment before his knock. Giving Natalie a hard glare, Madalyn flung open the door.

"There you are—hey, Miss Natalie, good to see you up. Jean brought by some cobbler from his *mamm*. Come on out and help us eat it while it's hot."

"Thank you, Papa Lobo," Madalyn said, grateful for the interruption. She didn't look behind her to see if Natalie was coming or not. She wasn't sure she *cared* whether Natalie was coming or not. She had been so worried about how to have a hard conversation with Natalie, and now . . .

In the kitchen, Doc was seated at the table with a cup of tea—he never drank Papa Lobo's strong black coffee—and a bowl of peach cobbler topped by rapidly melting vanilla ice cream. Jean sat a little way down from him with his face practically in his bowl. Madalyn sniffed the scents of cinnamon and peaches and sighed appreciatively. "Mmm."

"This cobbler is some good stuff," Doc said, setting down his spoon. "Who's your friend?"

Madalyn twisted to see Natalie hovering uncertainly behind her. Madalyn felt snarly and ungracious, and it showed in her introduction. "Dr. Buchannan, this is my *classmate* Natalie Parry. Natalie, this is my *friend* Doc Buchannan. And I know you remember when you met my friend Jean Duval at the drugstore," she added, narrowing her eyes.

Natalie's face went pink.

Doc smiled and saluted Natalie with his mug of tea. Jean, who was hunched over his bowl, nodded and said, "What's up?"—or, really, "Sup?" since most of the sentence was chewed up with his food. Doc looked at Jean and shook his head.

"Forgive our manners, ladies, but in Jean's defense, his mother is a wonderful cook."

"What? I said hi," Jean protested, wiping his mouth with the back of his hand.

"With half the cobbler in your mouth," Madalyn muttered, which made Doc slap his knee and laugh.

"She's got you there, son."

As Papa Lobo was bustling around, asking Natalie if she wanted ice cream, Madalyn sat down next to Jean, scooting her chair away from where Natalie sat at the foot of the table. Papa Lobo set Natalie's ice-cream-topped cobbler in front of her.

"You sure you don't want something else, Natalie?" Madalyn asked, still feeling out of sorts. "I'm sure *Annica* wouldn't like you eating this for breakfast."

"Why not? It's just fruit," Papa Lobo said, setting down Madalyn's bowl of cobbler. Hers had no ice cream. "Fruit and milk. A healthy meal."

Madalyn rolled her eyes at Natalie's giggle. "Whatever. Did you find the wall stuff, Papa Lobo?"

Papa Lobo settled himself at the table with a heaping bowl of cobbler, ice cream, and his black coffee.

"Yes, ma'am. You going to get some work done today?"

"As soon as I finish. I'll fill the holes down close to the floor and let Jean do the holes up top. We could get the whole thing done today, maybe—everything but the wallpaper."

"Um, are you building something?" Natalie asked hesitantly.

"Jean and I have a project with Papa Lobo—it's nothing *Annica* would want you working on," Madalyn said, her temper stinging through her voice like icy hail.

At that, Papa Lobo, Doc, and Jean all looked up, glancing in surprise from Madalyn to Natalie. Madalyn's face grew warm, and she stared at her cobbler. She waited for Papa Lobo to say something to her like Mom and Daddy would have. Instead, it was Jean who spoke.

"What's the matter, Mads, you don't want Natalie to see my inheritance?"

"What?" Madalyn scowled in confusion.

"You know Papa Lobo is going to leave me all those roosters when he dies," Jean said, and grinned at Papa Lobo, who gave an incredulous huff. "Since I've been doing all the work—"

"Oh, *whatever*, Jean. I know I did at least half the

work, so you can get over—"

"Neither of you are getting my cockerels," Papa Lobo interrupted. "You children eat up and stop bickering. Doc, you want to give me the sports page?"

"You see how he is?" Jean complained, standing up to rinse his bowl. "He reads and I work. It's child labor, that's what this is."

"It's a crying shame, isn't it?" Papa Lobo said, opening the sports section.

"It sure is," Doc said, and had another bite of cobbler. "Lo, what's a five-letter word for lazy? I'm trying to do the crossword."

Even Madalyn laughed at that, while Jean sighed loudly. "I see how it's going to be. Well, come on, Mads, hurry up. Josh wants to play *Skywatch* at two, and if you want to finish all the spackling today, we've got to get a move on."

Madalyn hurriedly shoveled food into her mouth. She was surprised to find Natalie trying to speed up as well. "Don't rush," Madalyn said in a low voice. "You don't have to do anything."

"I can help," Natalie insisted.

"Nah, wouldn't want to mess up your nails," Madalyn said, and stood up, pretending not to see Natalie's hurt expression.

"She can tape all the boxes together and help pack up the roosters," Jean interrupted, giving Madalyn a scowl. "There's a lot of stuff she can do that won't wreck her nails."

Madalyn shrugged. "Whatever. Let's go."

"You all right, *ché*?" Papa Lobo asked, fingers brushing Madalyn's arm as she passed.

"I'm fine," Madalyn said. "Oh—I tried calling Mom, but it just rang."

Papa Lobo sighed. "Those cell phone towers are a mess right now." He peered at Madalyn over his reading glasses. "That's no excuse not to be sweet, *mamzél*, is it? You just hold on. Your *mamm* is going to come through just fine."

Madalyn shrugged a shoulder because she couldn't speak around the lump in her throat. She'd expected that little talking-to, and she knew it seemed like she deserved it, but she wanted to explain what Natalie had said and what she'd done. It wasn't fair!

Just then, from the front room Jean let out a muffled exclamation.

"What?" Papa Lobo called, rising to take Natalie's bowl when she stood up to rinse it.

"Mrs. Baylor just fell," Jean hollered.

Doc immediately heaved to his feet, grabbing for

his cane. "She get up yet?"

Madalyn darted down the hall toward the window. "Is she still working in the garden?"

"She's kind of sitting up, still coughing," Jean reported, going to the front door. He hesitated.

"Does she need help? What are you waiting for? Go!" Madalyn said, trying to push him out of the way.

"Wait," Jean said, nudging Madalyn back. "We need Doc. Mrs. Baylor . . . she kinda doesn't like me, remember? If I go out there, she'll probably have a heart attack."

"I'll go," Madalyn said. "She was coughing before, Jean. She needs to be inside."

"That old house doesn't have any central air," Papa Lobo said, hurrying forward with his bandanna in hand. "Hard to keep the smoke out without that. Madalyn, go get some ice packs in case she's got a bruise. Doc, clear off the sofa, and I'll bring her back to you. Jean, come with me."

Papa Lobo and Jean slipped out the door. Madalyn dashed for the kitchen, snatching a dish towel to press over her face as she hurried out to the back porch and the deep freeze. Madalyn dug until she found the blue ice packs, then hurried back inside. She could hear Doc talking in the front room as she came in.

"Yep, we'll just push that table back—that's the way."

"Do you want a blanket?" Madalyn asked, dumping the cold packs on a sheet-covered end table.

"Thank you, Madalyn, that's a good idea. Natalie, let's move some of these boxes back out of the way—"

Madalyn was racing back with a blanket from the linen closet as Jean and Papa Lobo helped Mrs. Baylor into the entryway. Jean kicked the door closed, and Madalyn wrinkled her nose at the burning stench. How could Mrs. Baylor have been outside for so long? No wonder she had fallen over coughing.

Madalyn trailed after the group into the front room, feeling her own throat tighten as she heard the awful sound Mrs. Baylor was making. She pushed the blanket into Natalie's hands and backed away as Doc instructed them to help the old woman sit down on the couch. "Slow, even breaths, Edna—let's take slow, even breaths. Do you have your inhaler? No? Can I call Iris? Oh, she told me she was off to see her daughters today, didn't she? Never mind. Lo, call 9-1-1."

"I'm"—*wheeze*—"fine," Mrs. Baylor managed. Her copper-brown freckles stood out against her pale skin as she struggled to breathe.

"That's what you said before," Papa Lobo said, and

pulled out his phone.

"NO!" Mrs. Baylor croaked, and her wheezing got worse with the angry word.

"Calmly, Edna, you're making it worse," Doc said. "Try to relax and breathe."

"I can go to her house and get her inhaler," Jean offered, looking worriedly at Doc.

"I don't"—*wheeze*—"need your"—*wheeze*—"help," Mrs. Baylor said, glaring at him.

"Oh, Mrs. Baylor," Madalyn groaned, wringing her hands. She didn't need Jean's help? But that was ridiculous! Mrs. Baylor's breathing sounded like an old vacuum cleaner.

Papa Lobo sighed and put an arm around Jean's shoulders. "What Mrs. Baylor means, *fiyo*, is that she doesn't *want* to need our help." He narrowed his eyes at Mrs. Baylor. "Nobody ever wants to need help, but if they're smart, when they need help, they accept it."

Mrs. Baylor just looked away, blinking hard. Madalyn's heart ached. Mrs. Baylor seemed like she was stuck in her stubborn mood, just like Madalyn got stuck sometimes—but it was a terrible time to be stubborn.

"I could go," Natalie blurted. Madalyn blinked, startled. But she wasn't surprised when Mrs. Baylor scowled and shook her head.

"I don't"—*wheeze*—"know you," Mrs. Baylor rasped. "Why should I"—*wheeze*—"let you in"—*wheeze*—"my house?"

"More breathing, less talking," Doc said, his voice firm. "Breathe in through your nose and blow it out like you're going to whistle. One more, please. Lo, just call an ambulance."

"Ambulances charge you an arm and a leg," Papa Lobo pointed out calmly. "Probably why you said no, isn't that right, Mrs. B?" Papa Lobo leaned forward and looked at the old woman seriously. "Look, if your inhaler is in the house, let Madalyn and Natalie both go ahead and get it. You don't have time to play around, now. Tell us where to look or I'll have to call an ambulance."

Mrs. Baylor blinked her glaring, red-rimmed eyes at him, then, after a long pause, nodded stiffly, her narrow shoulders slumping.

Moments later, Madalyn and Natalie were in Madalyn's room, tying makeshift masks over their faces and putting on their shoes.

Natalie's expression was mutinous. "She doesn't deserve Mr. Lobo being nice. We're trying to *help*! I can't believe she was so rude to Jean, right to his face."

Madalyn gave Natalie an annoyed look. "What, it makes you better because you just thought bad stuff about Jean but didn't say it out loud?" she sniped, then grimaced at Natalie's expression. "Okay, sorry, that wasn't fair, but you *know* you don't have to be friends with someone to help them. And, anyway, Mrs. Baylor's acting rude right now, but that's on her, right? Mom says we don't have to be a mirror and reflect back people's bad attitudes."

"I guess," Natalie said doubtfully, and then they were at the front door.

Even though she was breathing in tiny sips, the smoke smell penetrated through the cloth mask over Madalyn's nose and mouth immediately. Doc had said not to run, but to hurry, so she speed walked across the street and through the gate into the beautiful front yard, Natalie at her side. Once inside, however, Madalyn paused, wishing she'd been invited to look at the gorgeous flowers on a better day. It was purely magical, like something from a magazine. The three-tiered cement fountain wasn't running now, but there were other special touches—little garden gnomes and fairy houses tucked at the base of the trees, windchimes and teacup birdfeeders, a graveled path winding from the front porch, and lavender, rosebushes, zinnias,

217

and intensely colored poppies swaying in the smoky breeze.

"Ooh," Natalie said, touching a peach-edged rose. "This is amazing."

"Yeah." Madalyn stopped a moment and took in the beauty brought to life by her difficult, complicated neighbor. Sighing, Madalyn forced herself to move. "We'd better hurry."

Even going as fast as they could, it took time to search an unfamiliar house. Mrs. Baylor was so rattled, she hadn't been able to quite remember where her inhaler was—it was either on her bedside table, or there was an extra one in the corner kitchen cabinet, maybe? After Madalyn searched three wrong cabinets, Natalie gave a cry of triumph.

"Got it," she said, grabbing the inhaler and a bottle of prescription pills from a cabinet near the hall. This time, Natalie led as they rounded the corner of the house and hurried across the street.

Mrs. Baylor held out her hand in a silent demand as Natalie came into the room. She didn't say a word of thanks, or even nod as she took the inhaler. She waved Doc away sharply as she set it between her lips, and Madalyn shook her head at the woman's attitude.

"Does she even care everyone's running around

to help her?" Madalyn muttered indignantly as they handed the bottle of pills off to Doc. Papa Lobo had made fresh coffee, and the smell pushed back some of the stink of the smoke.

"Probably not." Natalie braced herself against the wall and toed out of her shoes. "I don't know, Madalyn, maybe that's not the point. Maybe it's like you said—that the point is being the kind of people who do good things even when people don't deserve it—or care about it."

Madalyn shrugged and picked up her shoes, still grumpy. Sure, some people were able to be nice when nobody deserved it—people like priests, and doctors, and social workers. But Madalyn was just Madalyn, not a social worker like Mom, or a medical person like Doc. Maybe if Madalyn were older like them, she'd be less frustrated right now. She'd always know how to stay sunny and positive, even when situations were tense and people were sour or rude. She would never get stuck in a mood, and she would know how to talk with Natalie about how she felt.

Madalyn frowned thoughtfully as she watched Papa Lobo lean down and speak quietly to Mrs. Baylor. But wait—that wasn't right. Papa Lobo *had* been sour with Mrs. Baylor. He didn't always say the right thing, and from what Jean had said, the two of them had been stuck in their bad moods for *years*. Papa Lobo wasn't always sunny or positive, and he was older—much older! Still, he was here now, *doing* the right thing when it counted. Just like he'd said before, no matter what anybody else did, Papa Lobo paid attention to how *he* acted.

On the other side of the hall, Natalie took two steps forward, then stopped. She turned and faced Madalyn, swallowing nervously. "I need to say this again," she said, her voice quiet. "I'm sorry, Madalyn, really sorry. Last time someone got really, *really* mad at me, they didn't talk to me anymore ever again. When my mom got that mad at me, she made me live with Annica." Natalie swallowed and twisted her hands together. "I'm sorry I got so scared of you getting mad that I lied and made everything worse. Can you . . . Do you want to try to still be friends?"

Maybe you didn't have to be a nurse or a rabbi or another kind of person who always knew how to be nice. Maybe any kind of person could have a hard conversation with someone else if you weren't the only one who wanted to have it.

Madalyn looked Natalie in the eye and thought about what Mom had said about friendship practice.

"I need my friends to tell the truth, even if telling a lie is easier."

Natalie straightened and took a deep breath. "I can do that."

Madalyn chewed the side of her lip and nodded. "Okay. And I need friends who don't get scared if I get mad. I'll try not to hold grudges for a hundred years like Mrs. Baylor, but sometimes both of us will be mad, and we'll have to figure it out."

Natalie nodded once, looking shaky and determined. "Okay."

If Papa Lobo could do it, she could, too. Madalyn held out her hand for Natalie to shake. "Okay, then. We won't lie, and we'll talk to each other when things are hard. Let's try again."

Here Comes the Sun

Lunch was prepared with all hands working and music from Stevie Wonder playing on Papa Lobo's wireless speaker. The old man tapped his foot while keeping an eye on the meat and carefully cutting the seeds from a spicy green pepper so the tacos would have "a little kick." Madalyn was grating a big crumbly chunk of white cheddar and trying to move to the beat at the same time, which wasn't easy. Jean flipped the warming tortillas and washed the lettuce in between stealing shreds of cheese. Natalie sliced the skinny green onions and made neat tomato chunks. Madalyn had just moved the cheese out of Jean's reach for the second time when someone rang the doorbell three times in a row, then knocked urgently.

"Well, that's not Doc," Papa Lobo said, and paused with his knife in the air. Dr. Buchannan had taken Mrs. Baylor to the emergency room, and with so many people having bad reactions to the smoke, he said he wouldn't be back for hours.

"I'll get it," Jean and Madalyn said in unison, but Madalyn moved first, shooting Natalie a fake glare as she snuck a chunk of cheese to snack on. "I saw that," she warned, sliding her bare feet against the cool wood as she sashayed to the door. "Hands off my cheese, people!"

Madalyn opened the door, ready to say, "May I help you?" like Mom always wanted her to when she talked to strangers, but instead, when she saw the tall pale woman with the wrinkled skirt and the tired smudges under her eyes, she gasped, "Oh my gosh, *Annica*!"

The lady jerked back, and Madalyn slapped a hand over her big mouth. *Oops.* She'd never even met Natalie's sister but had basically just shouted in her face and called her by her first name like she thought she was a grown-up. "Sorry, Ms. Parry," Madalyn tried to explain, embarrassed. "Um—"

"Annica! Finally!" Natalie shouted, and pelted down the hall.

After that, Madalyn just got out of the way.

"It was rough," Annica said, wiping her mouth as she finished her story. After all the hugs and tears and thank-yous, Papa Lobo had invited Annica to join them for lunch. "The fire crossed the freeway, and everyone was trying to call 9-1-1, but none of us could get through. There we were, stuck between smoke and flames and the cars piled up behind us. If that man hadn't had a pair of wire cutters in his truck, I don't know what would have happened. He pulled his truck around, jumped out, and cut an opening in the fence that ran along the freeway. He held that fence back and started waving people over so everyone could drive to safety. We had to drive down a pretty steep hill, and my bumper got dinged up, but I made it."

"Man," Jean breathed, shaking his head. "I hope somebody got pictures."

Annica laughed. "I'm sure somebody did—just not me. I was too busy trying to pretend my dinky little car had four-wheel drive." Annica looked over at Papa Lobo, who was chewing his last bite of taco and sighed tiredly. "Thank you so much for opening your home to my sister and me. I'm so sorry to eat and run, Mr. Thomas, but I'm about to pass out. If you don't mind bringing Nat home—"

"No, I'm coming," Natalie said hurriedly, standing. "I'll just grab my stuff."

Madalyn left her food and followed Natalie to her room, where she watched as Natalie crammed her brush into her bag and looked around for anything she might have missed. She straightened and smiled at Madalyn.

"Thanks for picking me up this morning. I would have completely freaked without you."

"Thanks for keeping me company, too," Madalyn said as she fiddled with the hem of her shirt, then smiled a little shyly. "I'm glad your sister made it back. And even though everything was . . . kind of intense, I'm glad we got to hang out."

"Me too, and I know your mom will get here soon, too," Natalie said, stepping into the hall. "Next time I come over I'll bring my nail stuff again, okay? And we can make earrings, too."

In the entryway, Papa Lobo stood next to Annica and Jean, as Annica said thank you to everyone— again—and Natalie shook Papa Lobo's hand. "It was nice to finally meet you," she said, then she hesitated, and turned to Jean, adding, "Um, it was nice to see you again, Jean."

Madalyn thought she might have even meant it.

After the extra guests, it was quiet as they cleaned up lunch. Jean took the leftovers—for his mom, he said, but Madalyn knew better—and then left to play with his online friends. Papa Lobo turned on the dishwasher, then sat down in his recliner with the paper he'd never finished reading. He promptly dozed off. Madalyn was curled sleepily on her bed with her books when the black kitchen phone rang again.

Madalyn leapt up and dashed into the hall. She hovered, listening as Papa Lobo picked up the receiver, his eyes on her. "Thomas residence. Hello?"

"Macie! Didja get lost?" Papa Lobo let out a crack of laughter, and Madalyn leaned against the wall, her knees sagging in relief. "It's about time, girl, you had me worrying out here! Let me let you holler at your baby girl—c'mon over here, *ché*."

Madalyn was already reaching for the phone with both hands before Papa Lobo finished the words. "Mom! Are you all right? I was worried!" Madalyn said, and her voice was thick with the tears that wanted to come.

"So was I," Mom said, and gave a shaky laugh. "I'm

sorry it took all day, but they've rerouted a lot of roads and closed some others. I had to take three detours. I'm in a phone booth at a gas station, if you can believe that—my cell isn't working. I found a rest stop off the next exit—I'm just going to park the car in the shade and take a nap for a couple of hours, and then I'll get on the road again. There are a bunch of folks at the gas station who've been driving for hours like me. This has been a long, long day for everyone."

"I'll unfold the couch for you, so when you get here, all you'll have to do is lie down," Madalyn promised her. "Drive safe, Mama."

And now nothing was wrong—not the smoke and the smells, not their house maybe burning down, not losing all their clothes and things—nothing was wrong because family was all that mattered. As long as Mom and Daddy were coming, Madalyn was sure she would be okay. After all, hadn't she already done the hardest part? She'd weathered her best friend moving away and having to change schools. She'd learned she could live in a new place and get to know new family and survive, even if she did get homesick. She'd made new friends, almost lost a friend, and worked out how to be a better kind of friend. Sometimes things weren't all the way sunny, and pretty soon there would be other kinds of weather on the way—life was always going to be changing like that—but at least Madalyn had learned that she could deal with a few clouds, too.

She wasn't corny enough to use one of Mom's weather phrases out loud, but as she hung up the phone and looked out the window at the gray, smoky sky, Madalyn thought, "Finally—clear skies ahead."

Acknowledgments

Writing a book about conversations about race means *having* them, which is tricky. Hard conversations don't always go right the first time. Or the second time. Even when you're as old as I am. Sometimes you'll feel like, "Nope, not today, racism." And that's okay. We can get scared that having a conversation about race makes us look like bad people, and that can make us act angry, or not listen, or say the wrong things. I want to thank the people who keep trying anyway.

Thank you to those of you trying to be better anti-racist friends. Thank you to those of you working on your communities and families to be better at seeing what damage racism does. Thank you to those of you changing big things like laws and governments. All of us make a difference—even young folks. So, thank *you* for changing things, one hard conversation at a time.

Turn the page to start reading

1

Animal . . . Vegetable . . .
M-a-t-h-e-m-a-t-i-c-a-l

From Henri's journal

Reminders for the test in August

You've got time. Take it slow.

You know things. Let them show.

You've got this, Henrietta, go!

Fluorescent lights really, really sounded like bees, Henrietta decided, shifting in her seat. She'd never noticed them at her old school, but the lights at Alterra Junior/Senior High School made . . . a buzzy, rattly noise that no one else seemed to notice. Not the test teacher. Not the few other students spread out, staring at screens. Just Henrietta. The noise had been mostly okay during the reading portion of the test—Henri could read in a hurricane and not miss a word—but math . . . well, math was different.

Henrietta gnawed her bottom lip and squinted at the screen. Answer, answer, she needed to choose an answer . . . Sighing, she clicked (c), the answer closest to hers, then caught her pencil as it rolled off the table from her scratch paper. She scrubbed her hands against her denim shorts and glanced at the clock again. Had the hour hand moved forward toward the six? Did she have five more minutes or fifteen? Why didn't this school have digital clocks like everyone else?

Henrietta rubbed her face and breathed out a silent sigh as she faced the next question. Okay. She *knew* this one. She *did*. It just . . . was making her brain stop, somehow.

A pair of jeans costing $39.50 is on sale for 25 percent off. Of the following, which amount is closest to the sale price?

When Henri had cut the tags from the jeans Mom had bought her from O.N. downtown, they had only been twelve dollars. So, probably, nice jeans didn't cost $14.50.

Henri looked at the problem again. Percents were easy—all of them added up to a hundred. Usually. Mostly. Sometimes. Was she supposed to multiply first and then divide? Or . . . move the decimal over and *then* multiply? One place over was 10 percent—so that was $3.59—no, wait. Henrietta rubbed her eraser over the scratch paper hard enough to make a hole in it. Ugh.

Other people, she knew, could solve these problems in their heads, but no, Henrietta *always* had to do *all* the work—the multiplication and the adding and the carrying, *and* she had to count on her fingers and use scratch paper too, just in case. Math took *forever* because she was just never *sure* of where she stood with it. Math was like standing on the beach, near the waterline, as the waves snuck the sand out from beneath her feet. She always had to start over. Henri could almost hear her brother, Jordan, complaining, "Man, Henrietta, why you gotta always do everything the hard way?"

Because. It was the only way her brain even *sometimes* worked to get the right answer.

"Ten minutes," the test lady said.

Ten minutes!? Henrietta quickly clicked an answer, then rubbed her chest, suddenly out of breath. She had too many questions left.

"Please keep your eyes on your own work."

Henrietta jumped. The test lady was right behind her and gave her a pinched smile. Henrietta sighed, turning back to her computer. She wasn't trying to copy anyone, but she knew she didn't always look at her own screen—or her own paper. Mrs. Zablah, her old math teacher at the Vista School, had said that Henrietta looked up as if the answers were going to fall out of the sky.

Henrietta very much wished they would.

She'd known this test was going to be hard—math in regular life was hard enough. She swapped numbers in addresses, phone numbers, and zip codes. She couldn't always remember when she baked, if ½ or ¼ was larger—which sometimes led to some nasty cookies. And it had taken her until last summer to finally memorize all of her times tables to twelve. "Just focus," Mom was always saying. "Buckle down and work." If only Mom could see her now, Henrietta thought. Her whole body was working so hard she was sweating.

Hurriedly, Henri clicked the arrow to the next page. The test lady had said she could get partial credit for getting parts of problems right—so if Henri could get the first steps of a longer problem right, she might still get *some* credit. She'd do a few from the second page—that would work.

There are 18 boys and 20 girls on the school's student council. If a student council member is

selected at random to speak at the next assembly,
what is the probability . . .

Nope. She couldn't deal with random.

Jayson puts $300 in a savings account that earns
3 percent interest . . .

Oh no, more percentages. Henrietta's eyes skittered across the screen to the next question.

Hindy's Garage charges $30 for brakes and $25
per hour of service. If T is the total cost . . .

Henrietta shook her head. Problems with letters took too long.

Henrietta clicked the arrow for another page, then another. There was *nothing* left that she could do quickly. She had to do something—Henri gulped and then, as fast as she could, chose a letter for each of the problems left: (a), (b), (d), (c). School started next week, and she needed to have the best score she could. She clicked another random set of answers. (b), (a), (b), (d). She would have to take Math Essentials with a

Mrs. Eden or something, she already knew that, but if she just did more problems, maybe she could prove—

"Time," the test lady sang out cheerfully as the screen went gray and the test disappeared.

Henrietta swallowed, feeling her stomach heave.

Math fail. Again.

Henri's shoulders slumped as she picked up her bag and walked to the door, the low buzz of the fluorescent lights a chorus of disappointment echoing after her.

"Hey! Hen!"

Shuffling home from the bus stop, Henrietta didn't even notice her brother. It had taken her twice as long to get home, since somehow, she'd left school and gone the wrong way. She'd taken the first bus that had come to the stop, but it had been the 116 bus, and not the 61, which would have taken her four blocks and put her off at its first stop, half a street from her house. Instead, Henri had gone halfway around the city before she'd gotten the courage to ask the bus driver if she could get a transfer and get off.

"Henny!"

Ugh. Today was just *the* worst.

"Hen! Hen, where you been?" Jordan rhymed,

rolling up alongside her. The low rumble of his scooter had hidden itself beneath the roar of the bus engine.

Henrietta shrugged, chin sunk to her chest in misery. It was too hot to rhyme and too hot to answer nosy questions, especially after tests.

"Nothing to say, huh?" Jordan wiped the sweat off his forehead.

"I was at school," Henri finally answered, crossing a corner of the lawn as Jordan walked his scooter under the carport. "Taking a math test."

"Oh," Jordan said, his clowning falling away with his smile. "Sorry."

Henri shrugged. "It's fine. Where have you been?"

"Oak Park," Jordan said. He fumbled for the key to the shed where he locked his scooter and bumped Henri's shoulder. "Better get a move on. Almost time to eat."

"Yeah," Henri said, trying to find a smile. "Maybe Mom got ice cream."

Jordan laughed out loud. "Yeah. And maybe Dad's jokes are all funny too."

Henri half smiled. Mom was way too into healthy eating for ice cream. And Dad's jokes . . .

The screen squeaked a protest as it was pushed.

"Jordan. Mom said come set the table." Their sister Katherine's heart-shaped face and waterfall of colorful braids poked around the edge of the door. Henrietta glanced up to find Kat's sharp eyes on her face, a small frown pinching between her arched brows.

"Wait, Henrietta, what are *you* doing out here? Did you just get home? You're late."

Henrietta made a face. "It's *August*, Kat. It's not like it's dark."

"But you left school at *three*. You didn't take the wrong bus or something, did you?"

Henrietta scowled. "What's it to you?"

Kat looked pained. "But, Henri! I even told you where to stand. How could you take the wrong bus?"

Henrietta looked away, shame and embarrassed anger fizzing through her. "I figured it out, Katherine, so who cares? I—"

The slamming shed door interrupted Henri's rant. Jordan ducked around Henri and headed for the door. "Move," he told Kat.

"Make me," Kat shot back, stepping away, though not far enough. Jordan crowded through and knocked into her with his shoulder, making her stumble.

Katherine shoved him. "Jordan, quit!"

"I *told* you to move."

"You don't *own* the door."

"You don't own the door either," Jordan said mildly, then hollered. "Mom! When do we eat?"

Henrietta tried to duck around her bickering siblings, but Katherine caught her arm. "Wait, Henri—"

She jerked away, keeping her voice low. "What? I took the wrong bus, but I got home, Kat. End of story."

Katherine released her, looking offended. "I was *going* to say that I'd take the bus home from school with you sometimes. But you can't be depending on other people in seventh grade. You're going to have to figure out how to do things by yourself, Henri."

"I *know*," Henrietta said, gritting her teeth. "I did it today, didn't I? I got home. I don't need to depend on *you*."

"Yeah? Well, you do it anyway," Kat said, lips tightening.

"Whatever." Henri dodged her sister and stalked through the kitchen.

In her room, Henri flopped onto her desk chair and reached for the drawer that held her journaling pens. She opened one of her notebooks and began to doodle with a fat black marker, drawing a scribble of lines that looped into rounded-off squares. Jordan's teasing, laughing, rhyming all the time self she could deal with.

Mom sighing at her wasn't pleasant, but Henri could deal with that too—and Mom was too busy lately to do anything but sigh. Even Dad's jokes and long stories were just . . . Dad. But Katherine . . .

Ugh. *Katherine*.

She said she was trying to help, but just like those lights in the classroom, she was always rattling, buzzing, annoying Henrietta. Kat treated Henrietta less like a sister and more like a problem to be solved.

In curling letters, Henri wrote *I am* . . .

As she added spots of color to her words, in her head, she finished the sentence: *Not stupid. Not your problem. Not going to let you bother me.*

2

Changes and Challenges

From Henri's journal

September 4

Today, stress. Tomorrow, school.

Scared? I guess—but I'll be cool.

Three weeks later, it was the night before school started, and half of the bedroom Henrietta shared with Katherine looked like the closet had vomited. Henri's half, of course. Random piles of clothes and shoes sprawled all the way to the neat line of demarcation down the center of the room. Henri yanked a sleeve of a T-shirt back over the pastel yellow masking tape, then slumped against the wall, sighing. She couldn't figure out her outfit for school the next morning, and Katherine had already been snotty about the mess. "Could you just pick something? No offense, but nobody will even be looking at you!"

Sure, no offense. Henrietta wasn't *offended*. Except

for the fact that Katherine *knew* it wasn't about the clothes. It was about . . . everything.

Henrietta walked over to her dresser and stood on a small wooden stool to lift off the lid of the clear-glass terrarium on top. "Come here, Wil," she murmured as her black-and-white corn snake rose on muscular coils and surged into her hands. Everything was terrible, but at least she still had Wil Snakespeare.

Henrietta sat down on a pile of shoes and let Wil's cool body curl around her arm, his blunt head bumping up against her neck as he explored under the dim coil of her curls.

After Henri's disastrous math placement test, Katherine had started acting even weirder. She wouldn't answer questions about the school. She shut down when Henri tried to talk about teachers or classes Katherine remembered from seventh grade. She said things like, "Quit bothering me! I don't remember!" when Henri asked her about who graded the hardest and which teacher gave the most homework. Now school was starting tomorrow, and Henrietta was scared. Katherine was so determined to make Henri figure things out for herself that she wouldn't even answer simple questions? What had

Henri done to deserve that?

At least Mom was excited. She was taking a sabbatical from her job at the lab to finish the requirements for her doctorate. Before, with Henri's tuition at the Vista School, her parents couldn't afford for Mom not to work. Now maybe Mom wouldn't yell at Jordan so often for leaving on the lights, or remind Henri and Kat to pull the curtains in the afternoon to keep in the cool. Sure, Henri would still wear Kat's hand-me-downs, and Jordan would need to keep his job at the camera store, but with Henri at public school, it would work—*if* Henri could handle it.

Which she could.

"No, not my armpit," Henri muttered, collecting her pet from where he had threaded himself around her neck and was trekking down her T-shirt sleeve. She wound Wil around her arm again and stroked the black-and-white pattern of his tummy scales. She wished she had nothing better to do than explore interesting landscapes like Will did. Instead, she had to get ready for tomorrow and tidy up her half of the room before Katherine came home and stroked out at the mess again.

She hugged her snake instead. "Wil, this is going to be fine, right?"

The snake struggled, disinterested in her clutching grip.

Sighing, Henri got up and put Wil Snakespeare back into his terrarium. Tightening her ponytail, she put on her headphones and found music to help her start rehanging her clothes in the closet. Maybe tomorrow when she woke up, her outfits would look different.

Of course, before the first song was even halfway over, she heard her mother's distinctive *rat-a-tat-tat* knock. Henri leaned her head against the closet door with a *thunk*. She wondered if she could fake not hearing the knock, but she knew better.

Henri exhaled a sigh. "Yeah, Mom?"

The door pushed open. Her mother adjusted her gold-framed oval glasses and peered around at the messy floor. The careful crease of her khaki pants echoed her perfectly straight spine. "Is your little albino friend slinking around in here somewhere?"

Henrietta frowned. "Wil isn't albino. He has pigment; he just doesn't make any reds, so he's black, gray, and white instead of red, yellow, and orange. He's a-ne-ry-thristic." Henri said the long word carefully.

"Fine, yes, all right, Miss Zoology," her mother said,

waving a hand. "As long as he's safely locked up in that cage."

"He doesn't bite," Henrietta muttered.

"Well, that's good, because if he did, I'd bite *him*," her mother said, like she always did. Henrietta shook her head and groaned, like *she* always did. Mom's jokes were as bad as Dad's jokes.

Mom stepped a little farther into the room and frowned, her long-fingered hands landing on her hips. "What is going on with this mess, Henrietta? Your laundry is everywhere."

"Nothing's going on," Henrietta mumbled, gathering up an armload of shoes.

Her mother raised her eyebrows. "This doesn't look like nothing going on to me."

Henrietta shrugged and hung another shirt. She wished Mom would get to the point.

Her mother's voice was quiet. "Daddy tells me you're worried about tomorrow. Henrietta, you have nothing to worry about. Remember, no one can make you feel inferior without your consent."

"Yeah, Mom, I know," Henrietta said, wishing that Eleanor Roosevelt had kept that particular thought to herself. Henri wasn't feeling *inferior*. She was feeling nervous. Shaky. Intimidated.

Her mother took another step into Henrietta's room, glanced at Wil Snakespeare's cage, and took a step back. "Okay, well, Henrietta—tomorrow is going to be a big day, but it's going to be a good day. We've met with the school counselor; we've seen the accommodation and resource specialist. You have a resource room, with a desk and a chair and nonfluorescent lighting for study hall and tests. You'll have a large-screen laptop and a whiteboard and plenty of scratch paper. It's not the Vista School, but with the right attitude, we can make this work."

"I know, Mom, it's fine," Henrietta said, grabbing another hanger. "We have the right attitude. *I* do, anyway."

Mom sighed. "You know, Henrietta, I was one of a very few girls studying analytical chemistry in college—and there were only two Black girls in our entire chemistry department." Henrietta's mother smoothed a tendril of hair behind her ear. "They didn't think I was smart enough, Henrietta. They didn't think girls knew how to do math and science. But I didn't give up. They expected me to quit—but I kept surprising them."

"I know—" Henrietta began, but Mom wasn't done.

"That's all I want for you, Henrietta. You know

16

how to try. You've got the smarts. All you need is the tenacity to hold on, even when it's hard, even when you hate it, and keep going."

"But . . . but what if I really hate it?" Henrietta asked in a small voice. "What if I'm not smart enough? Do I have to go back to the Vista School?"

"Hen! Don't think about quitting before you start," her mother scolded, worry lines creasing her forehead. You'll make new friends and have a successful school year, but you'll have to dig in. You're going to have to figure out how to hold on, even when it gets hard, and not give up. That's what this year is about for both of us, right?"

Both of us? Mom was worried too? Henrietta swallowed. So she *did* have to figure things out this year, just like Katherine had said. It didn't matter if Katherine wouldn't help; if Henri didn't pull it together, she might have more than another math fail—she'd have an *everything* fail, and that wasn't happening. Henrietta wouldn't let it.

She nodded weakly. "All right, Mom. I'll try."

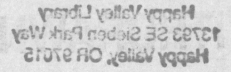

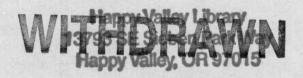